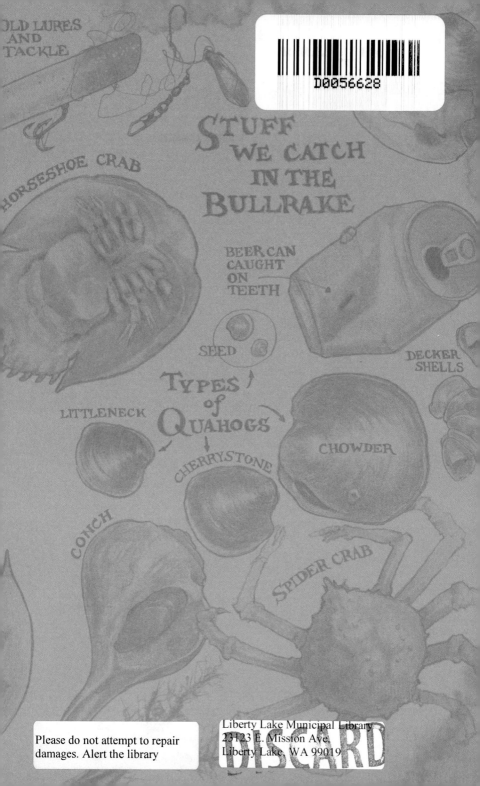

OLD LURES
AND
TACKLE

D0056628

STUFF
WE CATCH
IN THE
BULLRAKE

HORSESHOE CRAB

BEER CAN
CAUGHT
ON
TEETH

SEED

DECKER
SHELLS

TYPES
of
QUAHOGS

LITTLENECK

CHOWDER

CHERRYSTONE

CONCH

SPIDER CRAB

SWIM THAT ROCK

SWIM
THAT
ROCK

JOHN ROCCO
&
JAY PRIMIANO

CANDLEWICK PRESS

Copyright © 2014 by John Rocco and Jay Primiano
Illustrations copyright © 2014 by John Rocco

First edition 2014

Library of Congress Catalog Card Number 2013952797
ISBN 978-0-7636-6905-8

14 15 16 17 18 19 BVG 10 9 8 7 6 5 4 3 2 1

Printed in Berryville, VA, U.S.A.

This book was typeset in Galliard.

Candlewick Press
99 Dover Street
Somerville, Massachusetts 02144

visit us at www.candlewick.com

For Denise
J. R.

For my dad,
who made up stories for me every night
J. P.

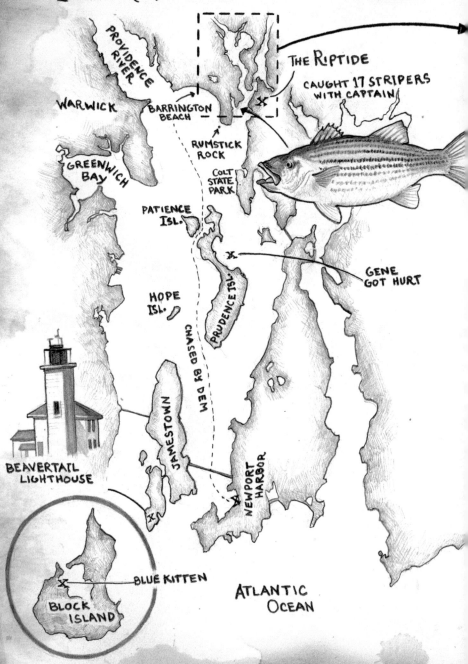

UPPER BAY TRIBUTARIES

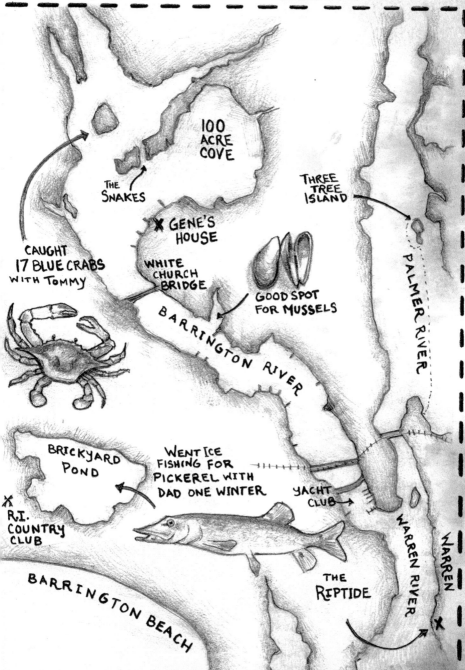

100 ACRE COVE

THE SNAKES

THREE TREE ISLAND

× GENE'S HOUSE

CAUGHT 17 BLUE CRABS WITH TOMMY

WHITE CHURCH BRIDGE

GOOD SPOT FOR MUSSELS

PALMER RIVER

BARRINGTON RIVER

BRICKYARD POND

WENT ICE FISHING FOR PICKEREL WITH DAD ONE WINTER

YACHT CLUB

× R.I. COUNTRY CLUB

WARREN RIVER

WARREN

THE RIPTIDE

BARRINGTON BEACH

1

WALKING THE PLANKS

Wednesday afternoon, August 11

Presumed dead does not mean dead. They didn't find his body.

That's why I am walking down the street in the middle of a category 3 hurricane with a six-inch knife in my pocket. I'm trying to find the guy I saw this morning who used it to stab a fifty-dollar bill into our fence post. *He knows something. It can't be a coincidence that the knife had my dad's initials. There's no way.*

The signs on Main Street twist and wobble, sounding like steel drums as the storefront awnings slap and shake in the wind. The sidewalk seems to move beneath my feet while my black poncho sets sail. It's pushing me back, saying, *Go home, Jake.*

I'm not exactly sure where to look for him, but my guess is that he's sitting in Muldoon's Bar. That's where all the fishermen go when they're not fishing. The street in front of the bar is lined with pickup trucks, and as I get closer, a couple guys stumble out, pull on their rain slicks, and stagger away. I can't see a thing as I peer through the porthole window on the front door. I push open the door, and the smell of smoke and vomit blows past my face into the surging winds behind me. It's dark inside, and the only light comes from red bulbs and a flickering neon beer sign hanging on the far wall. I can see dark bodies hunched over the bar like a row of black crows on a telephone wire.

The last dark shape lifts his head from his drink. Looking over his shoulder, he nods as if he's been waiting for me.

"Water's up?" he questions.

"Yup, almost in the cellar of the diner," I say nervously. I don't know exactly what I'm expecting him to do, or what he wants me to do, but I find myself just standing there. I guess I figure I owe the guy; he did give me a fifty and the knife with my dad's initials on it. He told me to come find him when the water came up, so that's what I'm doing.

He tosses the glass of beer back. It drizzles from the side of his mouth. Wiping his face on his shirtsleeve, he gets up from the barstool, which falls backward to the floor with a loud crack.

"Get in the truck," he says, pointing to the door.

"I . . . I don't know."

"Know what?" he snaps, throwing crumpled bills onto the bar.

I know I shouldn't get in some stranger's truck, but I figure it must be an emergency with the hurricane and all. None of these other guys are acting as if this is weird, and they must know this guy.

I'm thinking all this as I find myself in the front seat. The stranger climbs into the driver's seat. He's wearing black rubber boots, worn jeans, and a red flannel shirt that hangs on him like a wet blanket. It's weird that his shirt is buttoned all the way up, like he's hiding something. Black hair is matted across his forehead, making his pale, sharp features look like they were cut from gray marble.

"Where we going?"

"We got some business to do." His voice sounds like a shaken bag of rusty nails.

"My name is Jake, by the way. Jake Cole." I'm holding his knife with the initials out for him to see. The *J* and *C* pearl inlay shine from the flickering streetlamp.

"I know your name, kid." He glances down at the knife. "Keep it."

"What do I call you?" I'm wondering if his initials are J. C. too.

"Just call me Captain."

I want to ask him more about the knife and if he knows my dad and how he got the knife and why he gave it to me, but my jaw feels locked up. Stuffing the knife into my jeans, I look for the seat belt.

The stranger stomps his foot on the accelerator, and the diesel truck rattles down the street toward Charon's Dock. The dock, or what remains of it, is attached to the old oyster-shucking house, and even on a good day you take your life in your hands just walking on it. The pilings are all crooked and worn down at the waterline, fangs biting into the water. The whole mess has been trying to fall into the river for years, but some of the local fishermen keep knocking nails into it and adding new boards so they don't lose their access to the river.

The tires crunch to a halt on the shells at the edge of the dock, and I look over at Captain, wondering what we're doing here, especially in the middle of a hurricane. In the beam of the headlights, with every snap of the wiper blades, I can see white foam surging over the boards, forcing them to lift and sway. Suddenly, it clicks.

"Wait, you're not going out there. Are you?"

"Follow me!" Captain commands, and with a flick of his wrist, he shuts off the truck and leaps out. I am plunged into darkness.

I can't move. I'm frozen in the front seat. He's completely nuts if he thinks I'm going out there. I watch him as his dark silhouette bobs, limping quickly through the rain toward the dock.

Thwaak! A branch comes crashing down on the hood of the truck. Not a big branch; I don't think it even dents the hood, but the noise makes me jump right out of the seat. I pull the door handle and chase after him.

The rain lets up but the wind is still howling, and the salt spray is stinging my eyes as we walk the planks toward the end of the dock. Each step Captain takes causes the dock to lurch, so I have to time my steps with his to keep from getting tossed into the river. The five boats still tied to the dock pull and yank on their lines. To my right I can make out the forest of masts from all the dry-docked sailboats. The wind is tearing through them, moaning and wailing as it tries to rip them from their cradles.

"Ahghhh, nothing like a nice night out on the water," Captain yells at the wind and foam screaming down the Warren River. I can feel my heart pounding in my chest as I realize that he is going to get into one of these boats. He straddles two boards in front of a dark gray twenty-four-foot boat, which looks like a shark riding high on the waves. He's lifting the stern lines and swearing as the boat swings and heaves on its two anchors. He's driving a team of wild horses, pulling and stretching the anchor lines with arms that look like steel cables under a layer of ghost-white skin.

"Get on board, kid. Jump now!" Captain screams above the sound of wind and waves.

"What?" I say, questioning his sanity as a plank rips away and disappears into the rushing river. The dock groans menacingly and there is a spine-shaking, splintering *crack* as the boards beneath me begin to fall away.

"Do it now—just do it!"

I jump.

2

HURRICANE BOUNTY

Wednesday evening, August 11

"Get the anchor line!" Captain barks as he follows me and leaps aboard. *My first official orders.*

I stumble toward the bow, grab hold of the taut rope, and pull with everything I've got, but the last part of the anchor line is cinched tight on the cleat by the tremendous strain of the wind.

"It's stuck!" I yell.

Captain rushes forward, a huge machete in his hand, and slashes it through the air. The line pops like a guitar string. He races back to the steering post to goose the huge twin engines, and we blast out from the dock and into the raging river.

I look over my shoulder and can see my family's diner on the rising shoreline. The lights are on in the upstairs apartment, glowing like a lighthouse in the storm.

Everything is there, and I'm out here, in this boat, in this storm, with this nut job.

He motions for me to come behind the console as the boat jumps up and down in the swells. We pass a sunken sailboat at its mooring, bobbing and lifting, showing only her tethered bow and her mast leaning over at an odd angle. Captain punches the throttle forward, and the boat rises to the top of the five-foot waves, skipping along with the back end pounding like exploding dynamite. *This boat will definitely break in half.*

"I've seen worse!" Captain screams above the engine noise, and somehow I can't imagine a worse storm, but at this moment I plan on believing everything Captain says because my life is in his hands.

"Where are we going?" I ask, grabbing on to the console to get my balance.

"Strap in," he says, nodding to the metal post I'm leaning against. I look down, and there is a safety harness attached to it; I fumble with the latch, strapping in just as we lift into the sky. The engines scream as the boat catapults from wave to wave. Captain stands, holding on to the steering wheel, while I'm strapped to the post like a pirate lashed to the mast.

We find calmer waters in the mooring field at Stanley's Marina. The docks and boats are all jumbled in a pile. Some boats are upside down and sinking. It doesn't even seem real. Captain is steering quickly through the flotsam, dodging boats and debris as we fly by the yacht club and into the mouth of the Barrington River.

"Slow down! No wake zone!" Mr. Nathanson, the dockmaster, is waving his arm and yelling through a bullhorn. I can just make out his red hair and yellow rain slicks through the spray of our boat.

"He's got to be kidding. Has he looked around?" Captain shouts. I'm a little embarrassed as we speed past, and I try to hide my face behind the console. I know Mr. Nathanson because he eats at the Riptide. When he comes in for breakfast, he's always bragging about how athletic his kids are. *I'd like to see one of his kids out here, doing this.*

We continue to move up the river, past the cement bridge and then under the wooden trestle.

"Now what?" I yell over the roar of the engines.

"Salvaging." Captain's eyes are darting from port to starboard, searching the shoreline.

"Salvaging what?"

"Outboard motors. Listen, there's tons of rich kids too stupid to take their boats in when the storms hit; you'll see them all against the seawall and in the marsh just past Findley's Dock. We'll make some quick cash, and I'll have you home in a couple hours."

What is he talking about? Is this guy a thief? Captain

is crazy but the words "quick cash" continue to echo in my head.

The boat is running smoother now. The houses along the river are a blur, but I can see that most of their docks are all busted up. Trees and branches litter the shoreline.

The engines wind down, and I see Findley's Dock coming up in the distance, with its boats all twisted and upside down. Captain drives right up onto the marsh, lifts his toolbox from the locked cabinet, and hands me an adjustable wrench, two screwdrivers, and some large bolt cutters.

"You get the small engines. I'll get the big ones. Just cut the wires and don't worry about taking off the controls."

"You want me to steal engines?"

"It's not stealing, kid. It's right in the book of Maritime Salvage Law. It's called the Law of Finds." Captain is already disconnecting a medium-size outboard engine from the nearest boat. Pronouncing his words like a lawyer now, as though he's rehearsed this answer a hundred times, he says, "In the case of submerged and sunken vessels, when no owner exists or can be determined, title to abandoned property is given to the person who actually finds and takes possession of the property."

"But these boats aren't submerged or sunk," I say,

pointing to the dozen or so boats twisted up on the marsh.

"They will be soon enough. Now hurry up!"

I look at the boats, all in a mess, and I recognize my classmate Rich Ulner's boat. It's a brand-new fourteen-foot Boston Whaler with a twenty-five-horsepower engine he got as a present for not getting any F's on his report card. *What a snot.* I take my tools and slog through the marsh toward his boat. The wind and rain are whipping me. It takes all my effort to stay upright. I try to convince myself that the snot doesn't need the engine. He hardly uses this boat. His dad owns a whole chainsaw company, so he'll just end up getting him a new one anyway. *This is wicked wrong.*

"Let's go—get a move on!" Captain shouts.

I start fumbling with the bolts and drop my wrench into the eelgrass. I look over and Captain has already removed two forty-horsepower engines and placed them into his boat. His arms are moving frantically, pulling and cutting stuff. *He's a nut.* As I pick up the wrench, I see a flash of light, a searchlight, shining in the distance.

"Captain!" I yell out just loud enough to pierce the whipping winds and howl of the hurricane.

"What the hell are they doing this far up the river?" Captain stares out with murder in his eyes as he watches a Department of Environmental Management boat, towing a small distressed skiff up the river. We both stand very still as they pass by no more than a hundred yards away. The DEM are kind of like the coast guard, except they mainly make life difficult for fishermen. Most of us call them clam cops because they spend their time pestering all the quahoggers that work out on the bay.

Suddenly the spotlight swings over to us. We must look like two deer caught in headlights, standing there in the eelgrass in the middle of a hurricane. Captain is straining under the weight of the outboard engine in his arms. The DEM boat angles toward us.

"*Hey, you there!*" the clam cop yells through his bullhorn.

Captain drops the motor in the marsh and darts to his boat, trims the engines down, and motions for me to come. *I should just run up into the woods. I could just walk home.* The engine growls horrifically, and Captain points to me like he would to a dog, dragging his finger down to the deck of the boat.

"*Now,*" he says. I drop the tools, run over, and get on board.

The boat leaps from the marsh, then jerks to a stop as the engines hit bottom. I imagine the two stainless-steel props busting up the ground as the boat slowly moves backward away from shore. The propellers finally catch enough water to make it jump. Captain spins the wheel around and shoves the throttle full bore. The force throws me to the stern, and I bang up against the salvaged motors like a rag doll.

"Careful with those!" Captain barks.

I crawl to the leaning post and press my back against it, lifting myself upright. We head toward the White Church Bridge. The tide is so high I doubt we are going to fit under.

"Duck!" he barks, and I hit the deck, waiting for the boat to shatter against the bridge. Captain is laughing aloud when sparks fly from the metal bar over the console as it nicks the concrete bridge and we explode past it, out into Hundred Acre Cove.

We made it.

The rain is like cold needles piercing my face as the dark gray boat hauls butt. The DEM guys are chasing us. I can just make them out, with their lights flashing.

"Check it out, kid. We've got three thousand dollars' worth of motors behind us, and you get ten percent. Hold on."

I'm not sure what Captain is talking about, because I didn't actually put any engines in the boat, but I quickly do the math in my head, and three hundred bucks sounds pretty great—unless I'm in jail, of course. My head throbs and I want to jump overboard.

"I'm gonna bring 'em through the Snakes. They'll stove a hole in that piece-of-crap boat on the second turn!" Captain laughs.

The Snakes is a section of Hundred Acre Cove that connects two bodies of water through a marshy area. I used to go blue-crabbing up there, and I know about the massive rock right in the middle. It's covered in streaks of blue where other boats have hit it, and I'm thinking this guy is going to kill these cops, but he acts like it's a game of tag.

We hit the Snakes at fifty miles an hour. They're behind us now and close, and he's right; they're going too fast. Must be some new rookie clam cop driving, because I'm pretty sure they're not going to make the second turn. Captain slows just enough to miss the submerged rock. The sound of cracking fiberglass fills the air behind us as the DEM boat jumps out of the water and lands in the marsh. Captain throttles back as we watch the clam cops scramble out of their boat and immediately sink knee-deep in the soft mud.

"Never should have followed me that close." Captain laughs.

We turn around Crab Island and back up the west side of the cove to stay out of gunshot range. They may not be real cops, but they do carry guns, and I've heard they like to use them if the opportunity comes up. My knees are shaking. I'm wet and cold, and I feel like I'm going to pass out. Captain is squinting into the pelting rain with a crooked smile as we head back upriver.

"Ready for home?" he yells, and I puke all over the front of my poncho. "I'll take that as a yes!" He laughs.

"Is the storm over?" I ask, noticing the waves have diminished.

"We're in the eye," Captain says, as he brings us close to the little dock at the back side of the Riptide Diner.

"Good work, kid," he says as he pulls out a billfold almost as thick as it is wide. I notice it's tied closed with a rubber band; it reminds me of my own wad of cash in the cigar box under my bed. He pulls out three one-hundred-dollar bills and hands them to me. I reach out with a trembling hand, and he quickly pulls the bills back.

"We didn't do nothing wrong, kid. Law of Finds, remember." He hands me the cash. I don't say a word. I shove it in my pocket and jump out of the boat and onto the dock. Without looking back, I head straight up to the Riptide Diner. I hear the engines roar into the teeth of the storm behind me.

3

DIRTY MONEY

Wednesday night, August 11

The wind is still howling, and sheets of water make wakes across the road. I look up past the diner, and everybody has their windows all boarded up. Water Street is completely abandoned. I know that everyone's just trying to protect their storefronts from flying branches and stuff, but the thought crosses my mind that the whole town has given up and gone to live somewhere else.

I don't want to, but I slowly climb the wooden side stairs that lead up to our apartment. My dad built this place ten years ago. He used to be a shellfisherman, digging quahogs on the bay. He was one of the best. But working so hard on the water really screwed up his back, and when the doctor told him he had to stop digging, he decided to switch careers. Why he chose the restaurant business was always a mystery to my mom, but I know. He still wanted to be around it. He wanted to see the quahoggers off to work each morning.

We've been living above the Riptide Diner for almost three months now, in what used to be just a storage room and an office for my dad. When he went missing, and the bank took away our house on Wheaton Street, my mom and I moved in here. It's tiny and smells like bacon grease, but I can see the river from my bedroom window, and I can walk, or bike, anywhere I need to go.

The flickering blue-green light of the television washes over the cramped room. My mom is asleep on the couch, and she has one of Dad's sweaters balled up on her lap. Her rust-colored hair is coming loose from the bun on top of her head, and she's still wearing her white waitress uniform that's sprinkled with coffee and ketchup stains. She looks almost peaceful.

I don't want to talk to her right now, but she stirs when I shut the door.

"Hey, Jakey, what time is it?" She drags over the words slowly as she sits up.

"It's late," I say.

She looks out the rattling window at the pelting rain. "Thank God you're home. Weatherman says the hurricane is going to be a category two or maybe even three."

"Who boarded up the windows?" I ask.

"Trax did it before he left. Everybody's gone to the shelter at Warren High School. I think we should go too."

"I'm not going to Warren High! I'm not leaving the Riptide." My voice cracks. "I have to be here in case he comes home."

"In case *who* comes home, Jakey?" Her eyebrows scrunch together with concern. "Your father?"

My jaw tightens and I look away as she circles around the couch toward me.

"Oh, Jake, you have to let him go. He's gone. He's not coming back." She reaches out to put her arms on my shoulders and I step back.

"You don't know that!" I spit the words. "You don't know what happened for sure. You don't know *anything!"* I storm up the narrow stairs toward my room and slam the door.

I rip off my poncho and throw it on the floor, kick off my boots, and walk over to the yellowed newspaper articles taped to the wall above my bed. I've read the headlines a million times.

CAPSIZED BOAT FOUND OFF BLOCK ISLAND
RESCUE SEARCH CALLED OFF

My eyes lock on to a grainy picture of my dad standing in front of the diner. He's smiling proudly. It's a picture of the day he opened the diner, happier times. Above it reads: LOCAL FISHERMAN PRESUMED DEAD. I know what *presumed* means. I looked it up. It's just like *assumed,* and my dad always said, "Never assume anything."

I've read this article every night for the past six months, and I know every word by heart, and nowhere in it does it say John Cole is dead.

No one else thinks he's alive, even my mom; it's crazy. Being the only one, it feels like I'm carrying around this weight, this huge rock, and no one will even acknowledge it.

But they don't know him like I do. They don't know how well prepared he is, or what a good swimmer he is, or how well he knows every inch of the water out there and how he knows how to build a fire in the rain and make a lean-to, or any of that stuff. There are a million things that could have happened. He could have been kidnapped, or have amnesia, or he could have been picked up by some boat going to Cuba or some other island and he's recovering in some faraway hospital where they don't allow phone calls, or a million other things.

That's why I can't leave, not even in a hurricane.

I peel off my wet jeans and empty my pockets onto the dresser. Two quarters, some bag ties that I forgot were there, three one-hundred-dollar bills, my wallet with the fifty that's got a cut through it, and the knife.

Why didn't I ask Captain about the pocketknife? He must know something.

I throw on a dry pair of underwear and plop down on my bed. I've had the same bed since I was little. I took off the footboard last summer, and now I just let my feet hang off the end.

I pull out my dad's cigar box from underneath the bed. The pungent smell of tobacco reminds me of him, standing behind the Dumpster, puffing on a cigar and looking out over the river. That was his ritual at the end of each day. For the longest time I couldn't stand the smell. Now, I stick my face in the box and breathe deeply, wondering where he might be. *Is he smoking a cigar somewhere, thinking about me?*

I pull out a wad of bills tied together with a thick rubber band and count it out on my bed, two hundred and thirty-three dollars. It's all the money I've saved since I started working as a picker on Gene Hassard's quahogging boat. As a picker, I sort the quahogs, carry the bags, pull up the pole, and do just about anything else Gene needs me to do. He gave me the job because he's my Dad's best friend. I guess he wanted to look after me. Make sure I had someone to lean on or whatever, I don't know. Anyway, it's the best job I've ever had, and it feels great to be out on the water each day and not stuck in the diner from morning till night.

I take the three one-hundred-dollar bills and the fifty I got earlier from Captain and mix it in. I figure mixing this cash with the money I made with Gene will dilute it, make it less dirty. I count it again. The total comes to five hundred and eighty-three dollars.

The storm is on us now. I can feel the diner shaking and the attic ceiling seems like it's heaving. I'm wondering if my room will blow right off the top of this place.

I snap the box shut, slide it back under my bed, and shut my eyes.

Great. Only $9,417 to go.

4

THE RIPTIDE

Thursday morning, August 12

"We can always go live with Grandma," my mom says as I step down from my bedroom at five fifteen in the morning. She is sitting at the small round card table next to the stove and stabbing away at the keys of a calculator as if nothing happened last night.

"What do you think of that, Jake?" She persists in that way of hers that sounds all bubbly and fake. Every time she does the bills, she talks about giving up the diner, and I usually ignore it because I know she's not serious. But this time I know it's different.

"Is it because of yesterday?" I ask. "Is it because of those two guys that came in, the ones from the Italian Club?"

"What guys? What are you talking about, Jake?" She says this without looking up at me.

"Those two big guys, the ones with the satiny jackets with the Italian flags all over the back." I am angry now and pointing at the floor toward the diner below, where they were sitting yesterday morning. "I *heard* them. I heard everything! I heard about the ten thousand dollars we owe them, and how they are going to take the diner away if you don't pay them by the end of the month, and how some guy named Vito is going to turn this place into a nightclub and . . ."

"Wait, stop!" My mom reaches up and puts her hands on my shoulders. "Yes, okay." Her eyes are darting around, and I can tell she's thinking of how to put it to me. "It's true. We do owe those guys ten thousand dollars, and yes, if we don't pay them off soon they are going to repossess this place, but you have to understand, I'm tired of trying to keep this diner going, Jake. And you . . . you're working all the time; it's just not right. We can go live with Gram in Arizona," my mom continues, suddenly sounding all syrupy sweet. "I can get a job at Fry's grocery, and you can just, I don't know, do what other fourteen-year-old kids do."

I pull away from her. My jaw locks up and my ears start buzzing. I stare at a spot on the wall I want to put my fist through, the one covered in ugly wallpaper of local seaside vignettes. I imagine my fist pulverizing Beavertail Lighthouse to smithereens.

"Forget it, Mom. We're not moving to Arizona." I grunt through clenched teeth. "We're not going anywhere."

"Could you mumble a little louder, please?" my mom calls after me, but as I ignore her, she adds, "It's not your decision to make, young man."

Her voice trails off as I stomp my way down to the diner. The stairs are steep and narrow, and I have to put my size-thirteen feet sideways and scramble down like a crab. I forget to duck on the last step and crack my head against the doorjamb.

Great, another perfect start to the day.

Downstairs in the darkness, I wrestle the bucket out from behind the slop sink and fill it with scalding-hot water. I mop the floor and count tiles. Counting stuff calms me down, and there are seven hundred eighty red and black tiles on the floor of the Riptide. Light pours into the diner, and I can see that Trax is out front, taking the boards off the windows.

I finish mopping and wheel the bucket back into the kitchen. Through the screen I can see Tommy sitting on the back steps. Tommy is my best friend; he lives next door. He's always the first one here because he knows I'll give him free breakfast when Mom's not around. I watch as he lights match after match and flicks them into the sand at his feet. He doesn't smoke or anything, but he always has matches on him. He usually grabs a bunch from Deluca's Pharmacy when the lady behind the counter isn't looking. I can hear him whistling too as the matches flare up and then fizz out. I twist the lock and stick my head out the back door.

"You know arson is a crime. I think it's a felony."

Tommy quickly flicks his fingers, dropping the last match into the sand. Stuffing the empty matchbook into his pocket, he slaps me on the back and stumbles inside.

"Straighten up, Jake. You're turning into a wicked hunchback." Tommy is always telling me to straighten up because I slouch a lot. Partly because I don't want to keep cracking my head on doorjambs, and the other reason is I don't want to be such a freak. I am already six feet two inches if I stand up straight, and that is just way too tall for an eighth grader. This fall I'm going to be the tallest kid in the freshman class, and maybe in the whole school. *A total freak.*

In the last year, besides my dad going missing, losing our house, and all the other stuff, I had this crazy growth spurt. I grew so much my mom had to get me all new clothes. My feet were even busting out of my sneakers; it was like I suddenly became Hulk, only a tall, thinner, non-green version. It would be all right if I was a star basketball player or something, but I grew so fast that now I hardly have any control over my body. The kids at school started calling me Unco, which is short for uncoordinated, although it sounds a lot like *idiot* to me. The doctor says it'll be a while before I get used to my new size.

"That was a wicked storm last night, huh?" Tommy announces and heads into the kitchen. He doesn't really walk; he kind of bounces wherever he goes. He's a toe-walker.

I follow Tommy and want to tell him that I was out in the middle of that storm, speeding up the Barrington River in a stranger's boat. But I'm ashamed of what we did, so I lie. "I slept right through it."

This is getting worse. I just lied to my best friend.

At the milk dispenser, Tommy puts his head beneath the spigot and pushes the lever. "Aaaahhh." He wipes his chin on his shirtsleeve and pats the side of the black-and-white box. I grab the tray of ketchup bottles and head back toward the double doors. But Tommy gets there first, puts down his shoulder, and barges into the swinging doors like a football player—the skinniest football player you ever saw. Tommy could hide behind a fishing pole. He's been my best friend since kindergarten, and he probably weighs the same now as he did then, just two feet taller.

Tommy sits cross-legged in the last booth by the window, unscrewing all the caps to the saltshakers. Every fourth shaker, he throws some salt over his shoulder.

"Knock it off. I've got to clean that up."

"It's good luck." Tommy throws another pinch into the booth behind him.

"I don't need your luck; cut it out! If you want to help, then help. If not, then get out of here so I can get this crap done." I'm not really mad at Tommy, but I am mad in general and he's the only one around right now. I want to show him the knife and tell about my night, but I still don't. Not yet. Not until I can figure out who this Captain guy is and what he knows.

"So it's *Jerk* Cole this morning, huh? What's gotten into you, man? Did you forget to draw in your journal or something?" Tommy knows that'll usually get a laugh from me.

You see, when my dad went missing I was dealing with a lot of stuff; okay, not *stuff*. Anger.

That's what the therapist said: "Jake, you have some anger issues." She was right; I was pissed off and I had some serious issues. She told me to start journaling to let my feelings out. I didn't write down much, but I drew a lot in that journal, and it seemed to help. I still draw a little almost every night. I mainly draw the stuff I want to remember: things I used to do with my dad, things that I learn from Gene, things about quahogging.

Tommy bounces over to the counter to get the salt. "It's too bad you're so pissy, because I got some news that'll flip you out."

"What?" I say, annoyed. I start filling the saltshakers and carrying them around to the tables.

Tommy slaps both hands down on the counter and says, "The Mermaid is back."

"Yeah, and . . . ?" I say this like I don't really care, but I do feel a shiver of excitement. Janna Miller comes up from New York City every summer to spend time with her dad, Jay. I know Jay because he's a quahogger like Gene. I see him out on the water when I'm working on Gene's boat. Janna is tall and blond and tanned and probably the best-looking girl that ever was or ever will be on a quahogging boat. Jay used to bring her to the diner a lot and Tommy calls her the Mermaid, but not to her face. He's never actually gotten up the nerve to talk to her.

Tommy starts toe-walking around the diner, moving his hands in circles like he's crazy.

"You thought she was hot *last* summer. Wait till you see her now!" His eyebrows bounce up and down, and he's got that crooked smile going that he uses when he's really stoked about something.

"Dude, she's out of your league. Actually she's out of your universe."

"Not this summer. I'm going to catch me a mermaid!" Tommy grabs a butter knife from behind the counter and leans up against the wall, where my mom has been measuring me for years. It's covered with dozens of marks and dates and notes because she never lets me paint over it. Tommy places the knife above his head, presses against the wall, and turns around. He locates his own name from last month and starts writing on the wall with a ballpoint pen.

"Get this . . . I lost a pound and I gained a half inch. Come on, Jake, stand over here."

"I don't want to."

"Come on, Jake, it can't be that bad."

"No."

"Come on."

I shuffle over to the wall, mostly because I know Tommy won't stop pestering me until I do. He pushes my shoulders back and stands on his toes to get the knife flat on top of my head.

"Stop bending your knees, Jake. Stand up, stand up the whole way," he orders. I stand up. "Holy crap! You've grown eight inches since . . ." Tommy is squinting at the wall. "Since last July. If you keep it up, you're going to be the tallest kid in Warren." I quickly move away from the wall and knock the pen out of his hand before he gets a chance to write it down.

"I hate that stupid wall! It's like a billboard letting everyone know what a freak I am." I ball up my fist and punch the wall right where Tommy started writing my name. It dents just a little, and the rest of the damage is to my knuckles. It stings like crazy.

"Oooh. You showed that wall who's boss." Tommy moves in to inspect the dent. "Your mom's going to throw a fit."

"Who cares? She'll just take another Valium and get all fuzzy and forget it ever happened. Besides, she wants to give this place up and have us move in with Gram," I say, rubbing my knuckles. They're starting to swell into ripe cherries, but I feel calmer, as if I punched some of my anger straight into the wall.

"Wait, doesn't your grandmother live in Arizona?" Tommy asks.

"Phoenix, yeah. Doesn't that suck? I won't go. She can take that idea and shove it. My dad's coming back and I am going to be here when he does."

Tommy doesn't say anything, and I'm not sure if he thinks I'm nuts or what. We never talk about it. I plop down on one of the chrome stools in front of the counter, and Tommy does the same. We both sit there in silence. Tommy starts spinning around like he's a little kid. We both used to do that until we were dizzy, and then we would try to walk a straight line. My mom and dad would laugh like crazy. I can't spin anymore because my knees just jam into the counter.

"Darcy's here." Tommy points to the street, where Darcy Green is standing on the sidewalk, using the front window as a mirror while she ties her jet-black hair back into a ponytail. Darcy is in our grade, and she started working here last June. She is wearing her usual outfit: worn jeans, black Converse sneakers, and a long-sleeved Lycra shirt. The shirt is like something a gymnast might wear: skin-tight with sleeves that go all the way to her wrist. On top of that she always wears a T-shirt with the name of some obscure band that I've usually never heard of. Today it says THE RAMONES. I grab the keys from behind the register and let her in.

"What's up, Stretch?"

I only let Darcy call me that.

"Morning, Darce." I smile just a little as she glides past me toward the coffeemaker.

"Leaving us to go fishing again?" Darcy asks as she pulls the filters down from the shelf.

"It's quahogging. You always say going fishing, like I'm just messing around on a boat all day."

"Quahogging, of course." Darcy mocks, slapping her forehead with her palm. "Are you going *quahogging* today?"

"Yeah . . . no. I don't know. With the storm, we might not be going out for a few days. Gene will be here any minute."

She suddenly stops what she's doing and stares down at my right hand. "What happened to your hand?" Darcy grabs me by the wrist and drags me over to the ice machine.

"Jake got in an argument with the wall. The wall won." Tommy smiles and points to the small dent.

Darcy fills a dishrag with ice and presses it down onto my bruising knuckles. I wince and suck air between my teeth. The ice feels cool on one side, and Darcy's hand feels warm on my wrist. I look down and notice the shiny spiderweb of skin peeking out from her sleeve. I wonder what the rest looks like, if it's as bad as kids say. Some of them have said it looks like her arm was wrapped in bacon, and others like it was covered in Silly Putty. I've never seen it, so I don't know. It must be bad if she's wearing long sleeves in the middle of summer.

"Hold still, Stretch," Darcy says, pulling her sleeve down.

"Yes, doc." I wince.

"So why *are* you punching walls?"

When I hesitate, Tommy answers for me. "Mrs. C. told Jake that she was giving up the diner and they were going to move in with his gram in Phoenix."

"Give up the diner? She can't do that." Darcy's eyes are shooting back and forth. "I can't handle that!" She slams the ice machine door and storms through the kitchen and out back.

"I thought *I* was pissed. What's *her* problem?" I ask Tommy.

"Cut her some slack, Jake. This is like her place too. She's had to deal with a lot of crap, and now to add *this* . . ."

"I'm not *adding* anything."

"You remember what she was like before she started working here. The Riptide is her safe haven," Tommy says.

Darcy suddenly walks back in with a serious expression on her face, arms crossed. "So, what are we going to do?" she asks, slumping down on one of the stools at the counter.

"We?" I ask, joining her at the counter.

"Yeah, this affects all of us, Jake." Tommy says.

I don't have it in me right now to explain about the money we owe.

33

5

OPEN

Thursday morning, August 12

The three of us just sit on the stools, listening to Warren coming back to life outside the Riptide: chainsaws ripping through felled trees, the rattle of trucks hauling debris down Water Street, seagulls crying out for their breakfast, and the dull hum of fishing boats making their way up the river.

Suddenly the sound of my mom's footsteps coming down the stairs makes Darcy and Tommy jump off the stools like they're about to get detention.

"Morning, Mrs. C.," Darcy says while hurriedly wiping down tables. "Did the laundry come yet? This apron is getting funky."

"Check with Trax. I think it's delayed because of the storm."

"Hooo-weee! Here we go again!" On cue, Trax punches through the double doors and snaps a starched white apron around his waist. Trax is the only Native American that I know. Well, half Native American. His mother is Narragansett Indian and his father's Irish, so he's probably the only Indian with freckles. Now he's got his nose deep into the stainless-steel tins next to the grill, and I can hear him taking big whiffs.

Tommy quietly slips through the double doors to leave through the kitchen.

"Damn. Did you lose power last night? This stuff is rank." Trax starts dumping tins of food. Tomatoes, peppers, onions, and cubes of grayish-looking ham all go flying into the wastebin.

"What do you need? I'll go prep some more," I offer.

"Everything on the line. Gotta start fresh with all of it. Get choppin', Skipper." Trax whips my leg with a dishtowel and continues rummaging through the cooler, trying to find more victims to toss. In the kitchen, I find my mom already chopping onions.

"I heard," she says, wiping tears on the back of her hand. "We have to get that cooler looked at. God knows what that'll cost. I'm out of favors." She starts hacking away at another onion.

"Geez, Mom, get Gene to take a look at it. Do I have to think of everything?"

"I don't want to bother Gene with my problems. It's

nice enough that he pays you for going out on his boat every day."

"I work hard for that money, Mom," I say sharply.

"Oh, I know you do, Jake." She puts the knife down and leans heavily on the cutting board. "I'm sorry, I didn't mean it like that, it's just . . . it's just . . ." She looks up at me. Her eyes are red and streaming, and it's not just the onions. I can feel the small tug at the bottom of my stomach, telling me to put my arms around her and say it's okay and that everything is going to be all right. She sends out this vibe every so often, and I have learned to ignore it. I snip that invisible string that is trying to pull me close. I haven't hugged her or anyone else since Dad went missing, and I am not going to start now. Not today. Anyway, she's supposed to be the strong one, not me. She is supposed to tell *me* the diner is doing fine, and we can stay here forever, and Dad's coming home, and everything is going to be all right.

The kitchen is suddenly too hot and cramped.

"Morning!" Robin McCaphrey walks past me, and I follow her through the double doors as she kicks off her big yellow boots and strides in her bare feet over to the first booth, pulling sneakers out of her gigantic canvas purse.

"Don't leave those boots at the door, Robin."

"Yes, *Mo-o-om.*" Robin stretches out the word *Mom* the way she always does when she thinks my mom is treating her like a little kid. I think she's twenty-three, but I'm not sure.

Darcy and I pull the red vinyl padded chairs down off the tables, and every time she sets one down, she sort of slams it into place. I can tell she's pissed because she has this little wrinkle between her eyes that only shows up when she's upset. Tommy is right; she loves this place. Before she worked here, she used to sit by herself in the school lunchroom, hiding her face with her hoodie and never talking to anyone. It's because of the burn. The fire. Maybe she didn't want to have to tell one more person about how her house burned down and that her drunk father did it and how she was in therapy and why she never goes to the beach or swimming and how she doesn't go to gym class because she doesn't want to change her clothes in the locker room or any of those things. She's got her private stuff, just like me. But at the Riptide, she talks to everybody. Trax is like a big brother to her, and Robin's the sister she never had. And there's me.

After another twenty minutes of scurrying around, the five of us have managed to get the diner ready for the day. I karate-chop the main switch, and the lights above the booths flash on. Robin plugs in the OPEN sign that sits on the window ledge next to the door. I watch as the red glow of neon flickers to life and wonder how long we can keep this place going. *There's no way I'm moving to Arizona.*

6

THE AFTERMATH

Thursday morning, August 12

By 8 a.m. the diner is packed for the first time in months. Every quahogger I know is here. With the whole bay closed, they've got nothing better to do than come here, drink coffee, and talk about last night's hurricane. There are at least four men crammed into each booth, the counter is full, and guys are leaning against every open wall spot.

"Your savior is here." Trax cracks a smile and nods over to the front door. I spin around and there's Gene, taking off his salt-stained Red Sox hat and holding it to his chest with both hands like he just entered church. He nods over to me and I smile back.

Gene's not big like most quahoggers. In fact, if it weren't for his thick, calloused hands and his weathered, sun-freckled face, you'd think he had a desk job, like one of those real-estate guys who come in for the lunch special on Sundays. But I know Gene has never had a job like that. He's a quahogger through and through. Quahoggers have salt water in their veins and barnacles on their backs; that's what my dad always says. I must have salt water in my veins too; that's probably why I feel more at ease on the water and totally Unco on land.

Everybody's staring at the little TV that's attached to the wall above the register. Darcy is standing on a chair and wrapping aluminum foil around the coat hanger that is sticking out of the back.

"A little to the left."

"No, to the right."

"That's it right there." The fishermen yell out instructions.

"Where'd you get that crap antenna, dahlin'?" Mel Ghist asks, pointing with his coffee cup at the TV.

"I called in specialists from NASA . . . *daaaahlin'*." Darcy shoots back at him. Everyone applauds as the picture comes onto the screen. Darcy takes a bow and leaps from the chair.

The TV picture is crystal clear as a reporter shows the damage caused by Hurricane Marion. Shaky camera shots of trees ripped out of the ground, downed telephone poles, and capsized boats fill the screen. Dean Clements, the local postman, gives out a painful *Oooohhh!*

every time they show a damaged boat, almost as if it were his own, but he doesn't even own a dinghy. I'm half hiding behind the counter, pretending to be looking for something, crazy scared that they might show some of the boats that Captain and I "salvaged" last night. *They might even interview the DEM cops.*

"Can you believe this?" a fat guy named Red yells out as they show another overturned sailboat. "You'd think when those rich bastards heard the weather report, they'd have half a brain to pull their hundred-thousand-dollar sailboats outta the water."

"They've got them insured up the wazoo. They'll just buy another one tomorrow," Johnny Bennato says without even looking up from his paper.

"You sure that wasn't your boat, Johnny?" Red says with a nervous laugh that makes everyone uncomfortable.

"My sailboat has been on dry land since Saturday. I'm well-off, but I'm not an idiot."

Johnny Bennato's parents died in a plane crash and left him millions. He could spend the rest of his life on a beach somewhere, but instead he gets up early every morning and goes out digging quahogs on Narragansett Bay like the rest of us. He says he just likes the adventure of it. Most people don't understand why he does it, but I do.

"Are you just about done down there?" Trax is looking at me as I rearrange the coffee mugs for the third time. "You better get out there and help the girls, 'cause you're just getting in my way, Skipper."

"Yeah, sorry, Trax. I was just looking for something." I get up slowly and head out from behind the counter. I start making my way from table to table, clearing plates and placing them in a large black tub.

Darcy leans over and whispers into my ear. "Maybe all this extra business today will convince your mom to keep this place."

"Doubt it." Darcy doesn't know about the loan sharks from the Italian-American Club and the ten grand that's due by the end of the month. I want to pull her outside and tell her everything. I want to tell her I was out in the middle of that hurricane last night, stealing engines with some crazy dude who might know my dad. I don't know if she'll think I'm nuts or heroic or just plain stupid, but part of me really wants to tell her.

I push the thoughts of last night out of my brain and continue to clear tables. I notice Gene sitting alone at a small table near the jukebox where my mom usually sits when she does the ordering, and another pang of guilt rips through my gut. With all the commotion in the diner, I almost forgot he was there. I lift the black tub in my hands and give him a look that says *Too busy to talk now.* Gene adjusts his chair and lifts his mug. I acknowledge him and continue my rounds.

Then I happen to look outside. On the sidewalk, peering into the window of the diner, is a DEM officer, a clam cop. No, two of them! *Oh, crap!*

I dash back toward the kitchen, through the double doors, and place the tub down by the sink. *They figured it out. How did they know it was me last night?* My heart feels like it's going to burst from my chest.

I look through the order window, hiding between the slips hanging from the metal clip. One of the clam cops walks through the front door. His shoulders are so wide he almost has to step sideways. He looks to be almost my height, with a bald head, mustache, and a pinched, angry, red face. He's like the strongman from the circus, only wearing a khaki-green uniform and a gun holster. His partner, a scrawny, nervous, blond-haired guy, stays outside, pacing in front of the window. A hush of silence spreads through the diner as the bald-headed man walks over to the TV, watches for a second, and then clicks it off.

"Some storm last night," he says aloud to everyone in the diner, still curiously staring at the blank screen with his hand on the switch of the TV. He's close enough to me that I can almost read the numbers on his badge.

Above the badge, embroidered on his shirt, is the name DELVECCHIO. I'm thinking I should run out the back door, but if he already knows where I live, it's pointless to run. My knees are shaking so much I don't think I could run anyway.

"I know most of you in here are quahoggers." Delvecchio is looking around the diner, enjoying the attention as his hand slips away from the TV and he turns to his audience of diggers. "And most of you do the right thing . . ." He pauses for effect. "But some of you have been drifting the line, working in polluted waters. And that's just not nice. Some of you even have the nerve to work out there at night. *At night!*"

"Oh, give me a break," someone yells from the back.

"Don't worry," Delvecchio continues. "I won't be writing you any tickets anymore. No, my doctor said my tendonitis has been acting up, and writing all those tickets hasn't been helping. I've got a new pen." He pulls his gun from his holster and holds it up for everyone to see.

"You can't come in here and start threatening us with guns."

Delvecchio steps over to Charlie Crosby, sitting at the counter, and pats his back like an old friend. "I'm not threatening anybody, Charlie. I just want you to understand that there are some lines you don't cross. It's like the edge of this counter. One side, legal." Delvecchio slaps his hand down on the Formica. "But once you cross over that edge . . . I gotta write you up." He runs his hand over the edge and pats his gun for emphasis. "Say, is that an egg sandwich?"

"Yeah," Charlie says.

"Bacon?"

"Yeah."

Delvecchio lifts the bread, tosses the bacon to the side, and takes a huge bite. He continues to talk to Charlie between mouthfuls, loud enough for everyone to hear. "I heard you came in with twenty bags the other day. Twenty bags at eight thirty in the morning! You must get up pretty early in the morning, Charlie. How's the coffee here?"

"Good," Charlie says, his head hung low, looking at the floor.

Delvecchio takes a loud slurp from the coffee. He sets the mug down on the edge of the counter and lets it fall, spilling coffee onto Charlie's lap and smashing on the floor.

"Ow! What the hell?" Charlie jumps up, wiping the hot coffee off his pants.

"Oh, I'm sorry." Delvecchio sneers, throwing a few napkins at Charlie's chest. "I guess I didn't see where the *edge* of the counter was."

I'm shocked as my mom walks over to him with a

fresh pot of coffee held threateningly in her hand. She gets right in his face and says, "You either sit down and order some food or leave."

Delvecchio takes a long, hard look at my mom, tilting his head to the side. You can tell he doesn't want to back down, and she's not backing down either. They are inches apart. *Is he gonna shoot her? She's definitely over the line.* I'm scared for my mom, but kind of proud, too.

"You heard the lady." Suddenly Gene is standing next to her, nodding toward the door. "Don't make her repeat it."

Several other guys stand up, and soon everyone in the diner is on their feet. Delvecchio looks at his watch, and then throws his hands up in the air as if surrendering. "I'd love to stay. You make good coffee, but I have some other visits to make." Delvecchio backs up all the way to the door, and as he pushes through, he takes his gun and taps it twice against the bell above the entrance. "I'll be watching." He lets his voice trail off as he pulls the door closed. He grabs the other officer by the shoulder and shoves him toward their truck. Nobody says a word until they pull away.

I take a slow, deep breath and let out a long sigh of relief.

"All right, where were we?" I hear Robin yell out. "Who needs more coffee?"

Within seconds the debate turns back to the weather, as if someone has just turned up the volume again. Charlie's trying to explain his twenty-bag morning that brought Delvecchio on top of everyone. I grab the tub and head back into the diner to help out, snaking between tables and picking up dishes, glasses, and snippets of conversation along the way.

"There ain't no way they're gonna open Barrington Beach after this," Brendan Tooley says, pounding his fist on the table so his coffee cup jumps, making the spoon rattle around like an alarm clock.

"It was mainly wind blowin', not much rain to speak of," another voice calls out.

"They'll use any excuse to keep that beach closed," Brendan shouts back.

Johnny Bennato folds his paper and looks up now, much more interested in where this conversation is going. I can see that my mom, Darcy, and Robin aren't sure what they're talking about, but I am.

"I didn't know you quahoggers cared so much about going to the beach. Have you got some kind of sand-castle contest going on?" Darcy asks with a smirk as we meet up at the coffee machine.

"Not the *beach* beach." I look at her. "Barrington Beach. It's the hottest quahogging ground on the entire East Coast. Hasn't been opened up for quahogging in almost twenty years 'cause the Providence River has been dumping so much pollution into the bay over there. The littlenecks are stacked up on top of each other like candy in a gumball machine."

"Wow, Stretch, that's . . . really . . . exciting." Darcy is looking at me cross-eyed as she pushes the button on the coffee grinder.

"Yeah, I knew you wouldn't understand."

"It's not that," she says, laughing over the high-pitched grinder. "I just had this sudden twisted vision of all you guys down at the beach rubbing suntan lotion all over each other."

"You're one sick puppy, you know that?" I head back through the diner, trying my best not to trip and fall.

"I worked that beach in sixty-two," Ben Dunn shouts out above the noise. "Caught four thousand pounds of littlenecks in three hours. Sank my boat coming in. *Sank my boat!*" Ben shouts with his mouth full and spits food everywhere. I know he's never quahogged a day in his life, even though he's always in here talking about it. He's not homeless, but he sure looks that way in his stained sweatshirt, reeking of gasoline. I heard he even drinks shots of the stuff.

Everyone in the diner has an opinion on the fate of the beach, and you can barely hear anything over the noise. I'm just glad the television is off and they're not all staring at sunken boats.

"Wait a minute!" Brendan shouts out. "Bennato, you have a girlfriend over at the DEM. Can't you call her up and see what gives?"

"Oh, I don't know." Johnny holds his hands up in surrender. "That would just ruin the surprise."

Brendan fumbles deep into his front pocket, throws a coin onto Johnny's table, and says, "Make the call, Johnny!"

"Yeah, make the call!" others chime in. "Make the call. . . . Make the call. . . . Make the call!" I'm chanting with them. My mom shakes her head and moves from table to table with a pot of coffee in each hand.

Johnny moves slowly over to the pay phone with a look of defeat, smiling as he picks up the receiver. Everyone cheers. My Mom and Robin cheer, even though they still don't have any idea what they're cheering about.

As Johnny makes the call, the Riptide goes silent. The only sound is a lone spoon stirring in a coffee cup.

"Lisa Stewart, please." Johnny speaks calmly into the phone. "Yes, I'll hold."

After a few seconds of silence, Johnny puts a finger to his ear and turns his head away from the crowd. Nobody in the place dares to move while he murmurs into his cupped hand. Robin drops a dish from behind the counter, and it shatters as loud as a gunshot.

"*Soooorrry!*" Robin draws it out jokingly.

Johnny sadly places the phone back on its cradle. He puts both hands down on the back of the bench seat as if he's the boss, and now he has to tell everyone they've just been fired. Johnny looks around at all the faces mournfully.

"Well?" Brendan barks. "*Well?*"

"*Tuesday, August 24!*" Johnny shouts, breaking into a smile. "They tested the water this morning and said we are good to go as long as there isn't any more rain!"

The whole place erupts into cheers. Guys are slapping Johnny on the back and mussing up his hair. I look over at Gene, but he is still just stirring the coffee in his cup. I see a small smile creep onto his face, so subtle most people wouldn't even see it. But I know Gene well enough to know that he is smiling on the inside. I slam down into the chair across from him, drumming my hands on the table, excited about the news.

"What's got into you, Jake?" Gene's teasing me a bit with that soft bird voice of his, and I can barely hear him over the ecstatic chatter of the rest of the quahoggers.

"Are you kidding? Barrington Beach! This is what we've been waiting for." I let my voice go soft and birdlike too. "You're the best quahogger in this place. Heck, you're the best on the whole bay. We're going to crush 'em out there! Think of it, Gene, you and me at Barrington Beach!"

"Don't go getting your hopes up too high, Jake." Gene leans in close and moves his big, calloused hands onto the table. "There are a lot of quahogs out there, sure. But every guy with a boat and a rake will be there trying to make a payday, and just because we're all catching a bunch of quahogs doesn't mean people will be eating more of them." Gene must see the confused expression on my face. "The price is going to drop like a rock. We get twenty-four cents apiece now. Once that beach opens, we'll be lucky to get half that. Sure, Tuesday we will make a big score, but we're not just Tuesday quahoggers, Jake. You and me, we're six-day-a-week quahoggers, sometimes seven. That means we'll have to catch twice as many quahogs the rest of the week just to come out even with the low price and all."

I didn't think of it like that, and I can feel my shoulders slouch and my head crawl back into my chest like a turtle. I look around at all the other guys laughing and smiling about the beach like they just won the Rhode Island lottery. They don't think things through like Gene does.

Gene sips from his coffee and laughs. "We *will* slay 'em, though—I'm sure of that. Come with me for a minute, Jake. I want to go outside where it's quiet and we can talk." Gene puts two bucks under his coffee mug.

"Okay, that's cool, but I gotta get back and help out. . . ." My ears go hot and my palms get sweaty and I think he might ask me about last night. I know it's not likely he will, but the thought of it stings.

"It'll just take a second, come on."

I follow Gene through the blasts of high fives that are still rippling throughout the diner. Standing on the street, we both lean against his pickup truck. Gene uses his shirtsleeve to rub some dried mud off the tailgate.

"I've heard about your predicament." Gene stares at the pavement and kicks a few loose stones into the sewer grate. "Your mother told me about her debt, and I know what we're gonna do."

"You do?" I ask, surprised that my mother talked to Gene about it.

"Look, it sounds like you need to pay off these bums from the Italian Club ten grand by the end of the month in order to keep the diner, right? How much do you have?"

"Five hundred and eighty-three dollars." I shove my hand in my pocket and my fingers wrap around the knife. It feels hot in my hand.

"Hmmm. Look, Jake, I don't have much money right now either; I sank nearly everything into a diesel engine for the lobster boat and a new furnace for the house. This thing caught me at a bad time, but maybe we might be able to put a big dent in that ten grand if we work hard. Hell, I'll give you most of what we make, even the beach hit. I don't want to see you or your mom moving away, and I don't want the Riptide to close or turn into some nightclub. I like things the way they are." Gene laughs nervously. "You'll just have to work for free next summer, though."

I can't believe Gene is saying this, and I look down at the ground and scuff my feet along the pavement.

"Well, don't go crying about it. I'll pay you *something* next summer."

"It's not that. I mean . . . are you kidding me? Are you sure?"

"Sure, I'm sure."

"I'll make it up to you. I promise, Gene."

"You don't owe me anything, Jake. Just keep on doing the right things and this will all work out, trust me."

The dark shadow overcomes me. It's all bottled up inside, and now I want to tell Gene about Captain and the engines and the boat chase, but at the same time I don't want to disappoint him.

"Deal?" Gene holds out his hand.

"Deal." And just like that, I feel like things are going to be all right.

Gene pats me on the back and says, "I think we have an audience." I spin around and see a bunch of the guys looking at us from the window of the Riptide.

Brendan Tooley sticks his fat head out the door and yells, "You guys gonna hold hands all day?" An eruption of laughter spills out the door.

"Screw off, Tooley," Gene hollers back, and then says more quietly to me, "I'll see you early on Sunday when the bay opens back up. We'll go out and get you a payday."

Gene gets into his truck and pulls away.

I figure I am going to get teased when I get back inside, but I don't care. I know that Gene and I are going to catch more quahogs than anyone when the beach opens.

We'll save the diner.

7

HARD BOTTOM

Sunday morning, August 15

Today, I can finally get the heck out of the Riptide; it feels like the last day of school. I've been stuck working because Robin's been out sick, and with most of the Bay still closed, we've been busy. Being on dry land since last Wednesday has also made me a full-blown Unco. I've broken seven dishes and three mugs in the last two days, cracked my head against the doorjamb twice, and dropped a full bowl of oatmeal onto Johnny Bennato's lap. My mom threw a fit of apologies at him, but he just smiled and said, "No worries, it's all cool."

Part of it's been okay because Darcy and I have been working as a team and playing a few good pranks on each other—I am still trying to get the eggshells out of my sneakers.

I haven't told my mom about Gene helping us save the diner. I know she'll just get all weird on me and probably try to convince him not to help. She's like that. Lately it's like she just sucks all the air out of the room. I haven't really even spoken to her much since she mentioned moving to Gram's. I just do my work, then head straight to my room and journal or read till I fall asleep. I haven't seen Tommy either, because he's been visiting his cousins in Boston. It's probably a good thing; I've definitely been catching up on sleep.

This morning I got up wicked early and had the whole place mopped and set up before anyone else showed up, even Trax.

At six thirty sharp, Gene walks in, and I don't even let him sit down.

"I got your coffee right here. Let's go," I say, handing him a large Styrofoam cup and herding him toward the door.

"Yes, sir, boss." Gene laughs, turning on his heels.

"Geez Jakey, let the poor guy sit down and relax for a bit. What's the rush?" my mom calls after us.

"Gotta go, Maggie," Gene calls back over his shoulder. "Jake's running a tight schedule."

As we get to Gene's truck, I see Darcy walking down the sidewalk toward us.

"Morning, Gene." She smiles. "Stretch. You guys are heading out early."

Gene tips his hat and slides in behind the wheel. Darcy approaches me and whispers in my ear, "I'll convince your mom not to move."

I slide onto the bench seat on the passenger's side and roll down the window to smell the clean scent of shampoo from Darcy's hair.

"See you later, Darce. Thanks."

"Have fun." She continues down the street. I crank my head around and watch her leave as Gene pulls out onto the road.

"She's a great girl," Gene says. "I can see why you like her."

"What?" I quickly face forward and start turning the knobs on the radio, even though it hasn't worked in years. "No . . . no. What are you talking about?"

"Oh, okay. My mistake." I look over, and Gene's wearing that grin that makes the wrinkles in his cheeks look like gills.

As we pull into Gene's driveway, I hear the familiar sound of crunching shells. The smell of rotting clams burns my nose. Most people buy clamshells all cleaned and ready to go, but not Gene; he just throws broken clams right into his driveway for free. It looks the same, but it sure doesn't smell the same. I climb out of the truck and make my way down to the dock. I'm feeling great.

"Gotta grab some rain gear," Gene says, descending into his basement. Gene's boat, a Hawkline, has red topsides and a white fiberglass deck and is nineteen feet from bow to stern. It's part of my job to keep it clean. Right now, the deck is covered in broken spider crabs and seagull crap, and I dip one of the buckets over the side to begin washing it down. I see the culprit hovering off the bow in the morning breeze as if she were tethered.

"Thanks a lot, Jessy," I mutter, throwing a spider crab carcass at her. She makes shrill cry and hovers over to the dock piling and settles there. Most seagulls look the same to me, but the tangled knot of fishing line extending beneath her foot always gives her away. I wonder if it makes her Unco, too.

Gene rises from the basement with orange rain gear neatly folded under one arm. I watch him purse his lips and take a long look at the graying sky. I wonder if he's having second thoughts about going out. I hope not, because I've got to get off land as soon as possible. I need to be on open water.

"The dock lines are chafed. Remind me to pick up some rope from Stanley and splice that tomorrow." Gene throws the rain slicks under the bench seat behind the console. I make a mental note, but it may not stick because, as usual when I'm heading out onto the water, I am thinking about my dad. Maybe he's out there somewhere, getting ready to sail home.

Fifteen minutes later Gene is staring out at Barrington Beach as the Hawkline slides past Rumstick Rock. I know just what's on his mind. I am thinking the same thing. In less than ten days, that area of Narragansett Bay will be filled with a thousand boats and guys all trying to make a huge score to prove who's the best quahogger on the bay. But I know we're the best. Gene would never say that because he's not one to boast, but me, I'm busting at the seams and I want to show the world.

I look back from the console as the engine sputters, shakes, coughs, and finally, with a smoky shiver, goes dead. The Hawkline settles into a wave and begins a gentle bob in the early morning swell.

"Did you change the tank before we left?" Gene asks, then takes a swig from his coffee as I rush toward the tanks. Most of the time I can tell when the engine is running out of gas, and if I'm quick enough, I can switch out the black hose from the empty tank to the full one, pump the ball, and get the new gas flowing to the engine before it sputters out. But this time I was daydreaming about the beach and missed it altogether. Gene laughs as I frantically pump the rubber ball.

I feel the pressure in the ball build up, so I go over and put the throttle in neutral and begin to turn the key.

"Hold on." Gene sits down on the starboard rail with his legs crossed like he's playing cards with his buddies on a Friday night.

He's looking at the beach in the distance. "You see that area past the pavilion where it gets real green after the last house?" I take a spot close enough to hear him clearly. He's talking quiet now.

"Yeah, I see it." I sort of whisper too, even though there is not another boat within a half a mile of us. He's pointing to the Rhode Island Country Club. The last four holes of the golf course are right there on the water. I know because I caddied there a couple times last summer. *Worst job ever.*

"Okay, well, you see that first long hole, closest to the water?"

"Yeah, the seventeenth, I see right where you mean."

"Now come out about three hundred yards off that hole, and that's ten feet of water. It ranges from ten to twelve feet and then flattens out to sixteen. When you're in the sixteen-foot range, you're in the mud. The ten-foot range is like hard bottom." Gene takes his eyes off the shoreline and looks at me. He starts rubbing the calluses on his palm. "Anyone can catch the quahogs when you're tickling them from mud with a good drift, but can you catch them when the bottom is hard and thick with shells, and the quahogs are all huddled together tight?" Gene interlocks his fingers and squeezes them to make the point.

"I just figured it's all flat, and there's quahogs everywhere," I say.

"You still have to know what you're doing. Anyone can catch a day's pay, even more. But the guys that are gonna fill the boat with littlenecks will be prepared to stay all day and work anywhere, in any conditions. A lot of these guys out here will only work if the wind and the tide are just right, just the way they like it. We have to be better than that, because you know things aren't always the way we'd like them to be. When it's blowing hard, we work the chowders in the soft mud. When the tide is running, we work the hard bottom between the islands. Hell, we even worked that crazy drop-off near the channel south of Prudence. You remember that? I think we were using over seventy feet of heavy pole all pieced together."

"Yeah, they all laughed at us pulling up that pole until they saw you filling the bullrake every time." I'm looking at Gene now, and I can't believe how much he's talking. He never says this much, so I know he's telling me important stuff.

"It's the guys that play the tactical game, notice the breeze change, the switch of the tide, the ones that get out first, change the rake first. *That* will be the difference between a good day's pay and a month's pay when you're working the beach."

A month's pay would be real good right about now.

"Got it. So when it opens, we're going to work there off the seventeenth hole," I say, pointing to the shoreline. "Then when the wind picks up, we'll switch over to the mud farther east?"

"That's the plan, Jake. It's not all about what's going on above the surface of the water. Most of what will make or break a digger on game day is below the surface, at the bottom. You know how I can always tell whether I've caught an old bottle, or a rock, or a horseshoe crab? It's all about feel. When you have the rake in your hands, you may be in a boat, but you have to feel your way down to the end of that pole, where that rake is sitting on the bottom, in order to know what's really going on. That's where a quahogger's head needs to be."

Gene dumps the rest of his coffee in the water and stuffs his mug underneath the console. "You've seen those musclehead gym rats from Greenwich come out on the bay, all pumped up on steroids? They're much stronger than me, but they can't catch lunch, and that's because their heads are in the gym, not down at the bottom where the quahogs are."

He reaches behind himself, still sitting, and turns the key. The engine revs high like it's going to throw a rod, and then calms down as the excess fuel burns off. Gene stands at the wheel, knocks her into gear, and points the boat at Prudence Island. I settle into the seat behind him. I am smiling to myself now, because I know we will catch enough to pay off that whole debt.

The boat crawls to a halt about two hundred yards off the rocky shoreline of Prudence Island.

"Conditions are perfect. Drop the anchor." Gene looks at me with a slight nod, and I take the large grappling hook and lower it over the side, being careful not to let the ten-foot section of chain rattle against the boat. I let out enough rope so that the anchor will catch and tie it off.

"Got it."

Gene starts setting up the rake, and I put up the culling board and get my buckets in order. I can hear boats coming toward us from different angles and see that some boats are already working out west of here near Potter's Cove. I recognize most of them. Max Thiebold,

Frankie, Johnny Bennato, and Cholinski are all headed right at us like our boat is a magnet.

"Looks like we're getting jumped." Gene nods over to me, gesturing at the boats speeding at us.

"God, why can't they find their own spot?"

"You know what I say to that, Jake?"

"Yeah, I know. Change the things you can change, and don't worry about the rest."

"You're learning, Jake."

Gene sends the long pole into the water, hand over hand, until the rake at the end settles to the bottom. In one smooth motion, Gene takes the handle and gently turns the rake over so that the short metal teeth scratch into the sand. Gene's massive hands surround the handle as he moves rhythmically with the rake and pole, using all his motion and finesse to tickle quahogs from the hard bottom. I watch all his moves. I can hear the quahogs rattling, and the sound intensifies as the basket starts to fill up.

"Ready up." That's the command I love. I begin hauling up the thirty feet of pole, keeping perfect time with Gene. When the rake breaks the surface, it's full of littlenecks, right up to the teeth.

"Woo-hoo!" I shout.

"Keep it down, Jake. We're on 'em, and we don't

want these guys anchoring on top of us," Gene says as he quickly dumps the catch onto the culling board.

"It's too late for that." I'm looking out at the gathering crowd of boats now.

Gene goes about his business of filling the rake almost every time.

"Bags of five hundred; straight five-hundreds today, Jake." Gene leans over the culling board to make sure I'm paying attention to my counts. Sometimes we sell them to a New York buyer, and they only want four hundred and eighty to the bag. Today, Russell wants five-hundreds.

It's ten o'clock and we've already got three bags on board. I'm figuring if it doesn't get too windy this afternoon, we'll catch another five bags. Four thousand littlenecks, and at twenty-four cents apiece, that's nine hundred and sixty dollars. If we can do that every day, for the next ten days . . . I quickly let that thought drift by because I know that things won't always be as perfect as this morning. On the bay, things can change in a minute.

Counting is a big part of my job. It's all I ever do, counting quahogs, counting days, counting money. There are only two weeks until the end of the month and I've only saved five hundred and eighty-three dollars.

$9,417 to go.

Gene puts the rake down on the gunwale and reaches

for his plastic cooler lunch box. It looks like it's been through a war, all scratched up and dented. He snaps open a beer and takes some bread from a bag. I've already eaten my sandwich because this is the part I look forward to all day. When Gene takes lunch, I sometimes get to use the rake and keep what I catch.

"Am I going to work the rake while you have lunch?" I ask.

"Just promise me that you'll still go to college. Your mom made me promise I'd encourage you to go to college."

"Don't worry, Gene, I'm not even in high school yet."

"Yeah, but you'll be graduating before you know it, and when that day comes, I don't want to see you out here wrecking your hands on the end of a bullrake."

"I can't think about the future, only now: what's in front of me. Right? Isn't that what you say, Gene?"

I twist the handle of the rake over as it settles on the bottom. The rake's teeth crunch like they've landed on a granite driveway.

"Wow, that's some hard bottom."

"Concrete," Gene says with a mouthful of bologna.

I'm pulling back on the handle, and I can feel it right through to my own teeth. "It feels like I'm on a jackhammer."

"It has to feel like that some, but with less backward

movement. It's more about what you're doing with your hands. Tease them out of there; tickle them out."

"The rake feels full," I say.

"You've probably buried the sucker. Let me feel it." Gene puts half a bologna sandwich down on the gunwale and begins to rescue me. He gives the pole several sharp jerks to get it free from the hole I buried it in, and then starts to work his magic.

"Here, come close and watch my wrists and my knees; see the difference. It's a different stroke." As he is doing it, I can hear the quahogs going into the basket. I imagine I am down there, next to the rake, watching the teeth pull the quahogs from their hold and toss them into the back of the basket. It's a rhythmic sound, *ca-ching, ca-ching, ca-ching.* As more and more quahogs find their way into the back of the rake, the sound gets louder. Gene gives the handle back to me and I take over.

"Yeah, Jake, that's the sound we're looking for."

"Okay, I feel it."

Five minutes later I pull up the pole, and as the rake breaks the surface, it's half full of the prettiest shiny quahogs. To me they look like coins. I dump them onto the culling board and start to count in my head. I'm hoping Gene makes another sandwich.

"Try it again. You're doing good," Gene says, and I

hurl the rake out into the green water. I'm pulling hard because I am excited to catch a bunch more quahogs, but now the rake doesn't feel right. It doesn't sound right either.

Be patient; take your time. Don't muscle it; feel it.

I ease up and slowly begin to find that rhythm again. *Ca-ching, ca-ching, ca-ching.* The sound starts in faint, but it's beginning to build. I let out a little anchor line and keep going. I want to fill it to the teeth, just like Gene.

From the south, I see Dave Becker's boat coming over. His regular picker is not with him, and there's some new guy scrubbing down the side of Dave's boat with a long-handled brush as they approach. Becker likes his boat clean, real clean. Gene likes Becker because he's a young guy with a lot of talent, and he works hard every day. I like him because when he comes over to our boat, he always talks to me too, like I'm one of the guys.

"How you hittin' 'em?" Becker asks. I can see him counting our bags out of the corner of his eye. "Geez, Jake, you catch all them littlenecks?"

"Yup," I say straight-faced as I continue my *ca-ching, ca-ching.*

"What do you think of my new picker?" Becker smiles as he looks back at the other guy, who is frantically scrubbing down the deck of the boat.

"Morning, Bainsey," Gene says, giving the guy a slight nod.

As soon as he says "Bainsey," I recognize him. Jeff Baines. He's a short, muscular guy with this facial tic that makes him touch his chin to his shoulder every so often. He's been in the diner a few times. And I know for a fact that Gene doesn't like him because he's always spouting his mouth off about who caught what where and how much they caught. I'm wondering what he's doing on Becker's boat, and I think Gene's wondering the same thing.

"You heard what happened to my boat, right, Gene?" Bainsey asks, dropping the scrub brush and coming right up to the bow. "Came loose from its mooring in that storm, got trashed up the Barrington River."

I'm nervous now, because I'm wondering if his engine got salvaged as well.

"I think it was cut loose, that's what I think." Bainsey is twitching more than usual now. "Just before the damn beach opening! Can you believe that crap?"

"It's not right," Gene says.

"Don't feel bad for him, Gene." Becker spits into the water. "He's actually making more money working as my picker." Now they're all laughing, even Bainsey, and I'm relieved they aren't talking about missing engines.

The rake feels nearly full, but Gene always tells me never to pull up when someone's paying you a visit. I can barely move it anymore. *Forget it.* I slowly start to haul it up.

"Gene, I'm only covering for Dave's picker today. You want me to work the beach with you when it opens? It's gonna be a long day out there," Bainsey says.

Now I start to pull the rake up faster, because I'm ticked off. *What a jerk, to ask Gene right in front of me!* My rake is just breaking the surface, and I put all my muscles into shaking the sand and clay from the basket. The guys are all looking too, and the rake is three-quarters full of beautiful, shiny littlenecks.

"No, thanks, Bainsey, I got Jake here. He's all I need," Gene says, all proud.

"Woo-hoo! You got that straight! You stuffed it, Jake!" Becker says.

Now I'm feeling great, and even though it's real hot out, I've got goose bumps on my arms. I just pulled up a nearly full rake right in front of Becker and that jerk Bainsey.

Becker pushes off, and I can hear him yelling at Bainsey to get the bags ready and to pick up a shell from the bottom of the boat.

"Thanks, Gene," I say with a big grin.

"Don't worry about it. 'Sides, I never liked Bainsey one bit. That guy shoots his mouth off every time he catches more than a twenty shot. I'd have people camping on top of me every day if that guy ever came on board." He pauses and adds, "You and me, Jake, is all we ever need."

I'm actually busting because I have the feeling like my dad isn't really missing; he just picked up, left the diner, and is here with me, right now in Gene's body. I can feel my shoulders start to slouch and a fist-size lump growing in my throat. I can't seem to take a breath.

"I know what you're thinking, Jake. I miss him too. We all do."

8

SNAP

Sunday afternoon, August 15

"Hey, Gene, how come you never initiated me?"

"I don't know." Avoiding the question, Gene rolls his strained neck as he pushes the handle of the rake with his hips to keep the boat moving.

"C'mon. You remember, a few weeks ago with that kid, Randy. Billy Mac's new picker," I say, prompting his memory. "When Billy made him swim that huge rock over to that other skiff."

"Yeah, I remember. Poor kid nearly drowned in that raging moon tide that was bailing out between the islands." Gene hesitates, then says, "Listen, a lot of guys make their pickers do all kinds of crap like that, you know, to see if they have the stuff to make it out here on the bay."

"Yeah, but why didn't you ever initiate me?" I ask.

"Never believed in it. There's plenty of danger in this business already. The way I see it, a guy's initiated just about every day out here." A shadow crosses Gene's face. He stops digging and takes a long drink from the water bottle. "You've already got your own rock to swim, Jake," he says softly.

I know he's right.

"Let's pull up and try south of here," Gene says. I'm glad we're moving. He starts up the engine, and we head a about a half mile to the east and drop anchor.

When it's slow like this, I like to play a game with the shells. I find a target in the water, like a stick or some foam, and toss one half of a quahog shell into the air to see if it will settle like a Frisbee on the target. It's cool when it just floats there. Gene tries his luck at it too, and it becomes a contest to see who can get the best flight.

"That's a ten—that's a perfect ten. You gotta agree with me, Jake," Gene says, pleading with me after his last toss.

"No ten. It was okay, but check this out," I say as I toss one into the quickening breeze, and the shell pauses for a moment in the wind as if suspended. "Now *that's* the bomb," I say as the shell finally hits the water with a loud *plooooop*.

"All right, here we go." Gene sends a large shell into the air. Suddenly, like a boomerang, the shell comes flying back, and we both duck as it smashes into the console.

"What the hell was that?"

"The wind just shifted," Gene says, looking up to the sky, trying to gauge what's what. "We gotta pull up and get off this anchor. *Ready up!*" I scramble over and help pull the heavy rake from the bottom, but it seems stuck and the boat is twisting. Gene and I are working to free the rake while the pole is rising straight above our heads.

"Back away, Jake. Get to the bow!" he barks loudly as he takes the whole load himself. The pole is being carried by the wind in the opposite direction, and Gene is straining. The breeze suddenly picks up from the southeast, and now the pole's all twisted. I'm looking up at the handle with the Styrofoam buoy starting to wiggle back and forth, and all of a sudden there is a sickening *crack*. The second section of aluminum pole splinters right in the middle.

It seems to hang in midair for a split second.

I'm trying to warn Gene, but my lips are stuck together, and I can't get any words out as the two sections of pole drop straight down onto Gene's shoulder like a javelin. Gene crumples to the deck of the boat, and I'm on top of him immediately. Blood is draining from his shoulder, and he's already woozy and doesn't know where he is. We are at the back of the pack of boats, and the other guys don't see or hear any of this. They are probably all too busy dealing with this crazy wind.

I rip the shirt off my back and stuff it into the hole in

his shoulder. It immediately turns red. I pull the knife from my pocket and cut the shirt into long strips. I wrap Gene at the base of his neck, and tie it up underneath his opposite arm. He's bleeding straight through. I quickly pull up the anchor and start the engine.

"We got work to do; you get that rake; don't leave the rake, it's full . . . the sky's blue," Gene says, looking up from the deck, his legs all twisted in weird angles. I'm sure he's going to bleed out if I don't get him to the hospital.

"What do I do? What do I do?" I scream at him with my hands in his blood, pressing down on his shoulder. He's drifting in and out of consciousness. The deck is turning red.

Get the cut above his heart. That's what they said in first-aid class. I shove a pile of onion bags beneath his back and head and try to get him to sit up, but it's almost impossible. He's deadweight, and the boat is running around in circles while the blood mixes with the salt water and mud. I'm trying to yell for help, but all that's coming from my mouth is a dry squeal.

I finally manage to get Gene upright, and as the Hawkline makes another wide arc, I suddenly see Captain, sorting out his catch on the deck of his boat.

Unexpectedly, Gene reaches over with his good arm and grabs hold of my hand, the one still holding the knife. He's squinting and looking at the pearl skull. He looks like he's passing out and his eyes look half-dead.

"Where'd you get this?" Gene mumbles. "You're not supposed to . . ." Gene's eyes roll around in their sockets, and his arm goes limp.

"What?" I'm leaning right down into Gene's face so I can hear him, but he's passed out.

I bury the throttle and bounce us over to Captain's boat, turning at the last minute, making a wake and bumping into his port side.

"Easy, kid, what ya—" He stops midsentence when he sees Gene amidst the mud, quahogs, and blood. Captain jumps aboard, lifts Gene up onto his shoulder, and climbs back into his boat. I throw the anchor to the Hawkline, and just as I make the jump to Captain's boat, four hundred and seventy horsepower slams into gear, shifting everything on deck, including me, Gene, and the quahogs, all into a pile at the stern.

I'm up against Gene's chest, and I can feel his heart still beating. He's like a rag doll, resting among the shells and mud. I want to just lie here with him, be with him if he's going to die.

"You can't die, Gene, you can't die." I continue to press my hand into the soaked bandage to try and stop the flow of blood. I feel his hand move to cover mine. It's cold, but at least I know he's not dead. *He's looking out for me. He's holding my hand, and I know he's going to be all right. He's got to be all right.*

It seems like only a minute has passed, and we're already flying up the Providence River. The roar of the engines winds down as Captain pulls the boat up to a dock near the seawall. The cops are waiting, and there is an ambulance kicking up dust on the gravel road. Captain must have called on his radio because, like magic, they are all there. I'm all bloody now, keeping Gene's body warm with my own and gripping his hand, and all I'm saying is, "Hold on, Gene, hold on."

They get him on a stretcher, and I'm still holding his hand when the paramedics say, "You gotta let go, but you can come with him."

I slowly open my hand, all sticky with Gene's blood, and climb into the ambulance. I can see Captain, looking up at us from his boat at the dock. He's got the hose out, and he's washing his deck and quahogs and everything, engines shaking and smoking at the stern. He looks nervous with all the cops around, and he lets the lines loose from the dock and moves slowly out of the harbor, unnoticed, as they work on Gene. Before the doors shut, I catch one last glimpse of Captain's boat flying back out toward the bay.

The paramedics work quickly, putting an oxygen mask over Gene's face and sticking a needle into the vein in his arm. They attach a long hose to the needle that ends in a bag of clear liquid that they clip to a bar above Gene's head.

"What's that?" I ask

"Saline. Got to get his blood pressure up," the paramedic says.

"What's saline?"

"Salt water," the guy says.

I can't believe it. I start to snicker, but then I can't hold back and a laugh bursts out of my mouth. The guy is looking at me as if I'm crazy, and I probably look crazy too, with blood all over me, laughing my head off in the back of an ambulance. But I can't help thinking of what my dad always says about quahoggers. *They got salt water in their veins and barnacles on their backs.*

At the hospital, they rush Gene into surgery while I wait on a bench in the hallway. Because I'm not wearing a shirt and I'm covered in deep purple blotches of dried blood, nurses keep coming to me to ask if I'm okay.

Two hours later a doctor comes out and says, "Missed his carotid artery by inches. You did the right thing or your dad would have died." I don't respond. I too am getting Gene and my dad all mixed up in my head. It's a nice feeling, and I sit down on the floor and collapse because I'm so happy he isn't dead.

9

VISITING DAY

Monday morning, August 16

I slept right through the morning.

The sun is blazing, and it feels like a thousand degrees in my room.

"You okay?" My mom is standing in the doorway with her eyebrows all twisted together. I sit up and cover myself with a sheet.

"Yeah, I'm okay."

"He's going to survive, thanks to you, Jake," my mom says. "You never did tell me how you got him to the hospital," she says, pressing me.

"I got some help from another quahogger. I don't know him. Look, I don't really want to talk about it right now. What time is it?"

"It's ten thirty."

"Oh, damn. I gotta go." I scramble out of bed and start grabbing clothes, suddenly remembering Gene's boat. *Did the anchor hold? Are the quahogs rotting in this heat? Did it get salvaged?*

"Just because you work on a fishing boat doesn't mean you can talk like a sailor. Not in this house, young man."

"Sorry, Mom." I try squeezing past her, but she's blocking my way, holding out a thick manila envelope wrapped in duct tape. "Before you go running off again, do you want to explain this?"

I grab the envelope and turn it over. On the back, in thick black marker, it says *J. C.*

I know who left it.

"Someone slipped it through the mail slot some-time last night. It was there this morning when we were setting up," she says.

"It's from Tommy, just some tapes he bor-rowed." Not a very good lie, but I'm not wait-ing around to see if it works. I shoot out the door and down the back stairs as the screen door slams behind me.

Once I'm out of sight, down by the seawall, I pull out my knife and cut open the envelope. The silver tape is thick, but the blade glides through it to reveal a stack of twenty-dollar bills and a note.

Hawkline is tied up at Stanley's Marina. Sold out your quahogs. Took forty bucks for my trouble.

Captain

A wave of guilt washes over me when I remember thinking that Captain may have *salvaged* the Hawkline. I stuff the bills and the note in my pocket and head over to the bus stop on Main Street.

I climb onto the 11:03 bus to Providence. The air inside is stale and everyone looks tired. I find my way toward the back, slump down in the last seat, and before we leave Warren, I'm asleep.

I awaken and look outside and see Rhode Island Hospital. I jump out of my seat and bound toward the front of the bus.

"Excuse me! I need to get off. This is my stop. I need to get off!"

The bus squeaks and with a great hiss of air comes to a halt.

"All right, all right." The bus driver grins down at me from the big wide mirror above him. "Watch your step."

"What time does this bus go back to Warren?"

The driver hands me a small paper schedule. "You want to catch the Newport bus. Every hour on the half hour till six. "

"Thanks." I walk up the hill toward the hospital.

Inside, the sharp smell of cleaning products and the bright fluorescent lights immediately remind me of yesterday, of coming in with Gene on the stretcher, with people sticking things in his arms, and the blood and the plastic mask over his mouth. I get chills thinking about it.

I don't know what room he's in, and I just stare at all the signs on the walls. Multicolored lines on the floor zip off in all directions, and I'm standing there, trying to figure out which line will lead me to Gene.

"Can I help you?"

I look up from the floor, and standing in front of me is a young woman with blond hair tied up on top of her head and held in place by two ballpoint pens. She's wearing a blue cotton V-neck shirt covered with pins that have cartoon characters on them. "Are you visiting someone?" She says this all smiley, like she works at a theme park or something.

"Yeah, I'm here to see Gene," I say. She motions to a tall desk and slips behind it.

"Let's see, when was he brought in?" she asks while flipping through a metal binder.

"Last night. He was cut here," I say, pointing to the same spot on my own shoulder.

"What's his last name, sweetie?"

"Hassard," I say. "Gene Hassard."

"Yes, here it is. *Hassard, Gene.* He is in room four-fourteen." She points to the floor. "Follow the yellow line to the elevators and go up to the fourth floor."

"Yellow line," I repeat, staring down at the floor.

"Just like the yellow brick road," she says, rocking her head back and forth.

"Thanks."

Standing outside room 414, I can see the end of a metal bed and two lumps under a blanket that must be Gene's feet. I walk in and sit down in a chair next to him. Machines surround his bed, and they all have plastic tubes that snake their way into Gene. I'm surprised to see that his head is almost completely bandaged except for his eyes and his mouth, and his arm is in a cast up to his shoulder, with metal rods sticking out to hold his arm upright. He looks totally messed up. His eyes are closed. I just sit there for a minute, listening to the steady beeps coming from the machine to my left. I watch the lines that are tracing his heartbeat and think, *Just keep going. Don't you stop, you stupid line, don't stop.*

"Gene," I say softly, "It's me, Jake. I know you can't hear me, but I'm telling you, you can't die on me." I put both hands on the metal railing on the side of his bed. "You can't die, Gene."

"Who said anything about dying?" Gene says, but I can't even see his lips move. I stand up, looking around.

"Gene?"

"Over here, Jake." I look up to see the curtain on the other side of the bed move slightly. I dart around the curtain, and there's Gene smiling at me.

"Why did you do that?"

"I didn't do anything. You were the one over there, professing your undying love to a perfect stranger." Gene is laughing now, but it's making him wince.

"Gimme a break. I thought you were on your death-bed. You had me totally freaked." I know I shouldn't be, but I'm thinking about the beach. "So when are you getting out? What did the doctors say? You're going to be healed up enough to work Barrington Beach, right?"

"Slow down, Jake. The doctors say I should be out in a couple days, but I don't know about pulling that rake. The muscles in my neck and shoulder need to heal. They have to make sure there's no infection. They think it will be a few months if everything goes well."

"A few months? What are we going to do? The beach opens a week from tomorrow!" I'm totally freaking out. Gene and I making a huge score at the beach is all part of the plan. That's how it's supposed to work. That's how we were going to save the diner.

Gene puts his good hand on mine. "I'll make a couple of calls when I get out. Get you on Jay Miller's boat, or Dave Becker's. They're good guys, and they can catch a lot of quahogs. It'll be all right, Jake."

"But that's not it. They're not going to give me more than ten percent. They're not in on the plan." My voice is cracking, and I move away from the bed and look out the window at the Providence River. Gene must have forgotten. Maybe his brain is screwed up with all the drugs they're giving him. *What am I going to do?*

"Look, Jake, I'll be out in a couple days. We can get our heads straight and figure this thing out." I turn around, and Gene is pointing to the chair next to his bed. I go over and sit down.

"How did I get here, anyway?" Gene asks, and I don't know what to say. My mind starts racing. I don't want to tell Gene about Captain.

"Oh, yeah, well . . . I saw this really fast boat nearby, and I drove the Hawkline over, almost rammed into him, and he took us up the Providence River to where an ambulance was waiting and everything. He must have used a radio—I didn't see."

"Who was it?" Gene asks, and he's looking right at me now. I'm wondering if he remembers the knife. It's still in my pocket.

"I don't know who it was. Never saw him before.

84

Everything moved so fast once you got hurt." I reach into my pocket and pull out the pile of twenties and lay them on the tray that is suspended above Gene's legs.

Gene picks up the twenties with his good hand and looks it over. "You sold out? Where's the boat?"

"It's docked at Stanley's. I'll get it back to your dock this afternoon." I want to leave. I can't handle Gene's questions. "I gotta go, Gene. I have to help my mom with something. Call us when you get out, and we'll come pick you up." Shoving my hands in my pockets, I head toward the door as a nurse comes in, tapping her pen against the clipboard.

"And how are we feeling today?" she says in a sing-song way.

"Fine, fine." Gene responds dismissively, and just as I enter the hallway he calls me back. *Uh-oh, more questions.* I look back in the room and Gene is holding out his hand toward me. "Take this, Jake. I don't need it. You and your mom do."

"Thanks."

Stuffing the twenties back in my pocket, I practically jog out of there. I'm down the hall, into the elevator, and back in the lobby before I take a breath.

I rush into the men's room on the ground floor and splash my face with cold water. With both hands on the sink, I stare at the mirror, and the face staring back hardly even looks like me. My hair is bleached and wiry from the salt and sun, and there are puffy bags under my eyes. My chin and lips look almost like my dad's, except without any stubble. I stare at my mouth, and it seems like my dad is staring back at me.

"Is this part of the test?" I say to the reflection. I can feel the anger buzzing inside of me like a swarm of bees. "Did you let Gene get hurt? Was it because he was going to help me? Was that too easy? Why don't you just come home!" I want to shatter the mirror, but just then a doctor walks in and gives me the once-over, so I grab some paper towels, dry my face, and split.

By the time I get on the bus home, I'm ready to crawl under a rock and die. I shove my hand deep into my pocket, past the twenties, and feel the knife. I take it out and turn it over in my hand. The pearl skull shimmers in the sunlight coming through the bus window. My finger traces the initials on the back. I look up and notice this old lady staring at me over her knitting. She's probably thinking I'm going to hold up the bus with this jackknife, or carve my initials in the paneling of the back of the seat. I don't want to freak her out, so I just force a smile and slip the knife back in my pocket and stare out the window.

I can't catch a break.

10

THE DREAM

Tuesday morning, August 17

"Start bailing, Jake!" Gene barks.

Furiously I heave gallons of seawater out the window, but the bucket keeps getting smaller as the water continues to rise. That's when I realize I'm not in a boat at all. I'm standing in the Riptide Diner, knee-deep in water. Out the window through the fog, I see the outline of Prudence Island. I can't stop bailing. The diner is rocking and shifting with the waves. Plates and glasses shatter as they hit the stainless-steel countertop.

"We may be going down!" Gene screams into the howling wind as he pulls on the aluminum pole that shoots out the window into the black water. His rain gear is soaked with spray, and his hair is matted against his head. He has a crazy serious look in his eyes.

I drop the bucket, and it floats over to the stools by the counter and rocks between them like a pinball, and then sinks. My mom is behind the counter. She reminds me of a movie star, with her red hair tied in a bun with a small flower pinned to her blouse. She's humming while she wipes the counter, setting out silverware as if none of this is happening. The forks and knives shift with the roll of the waves and fall into the water at her feet, and she continues to hum and smile as she puts down new silverware in its place. I start to wade over to her when I hear Gene call me.

"Ready up!"

Instinctively I slosh over to his side and start pulling the long pole up through the window.

"The diner is sinking, Gene. Why are we still quahogging?"

"'Cause that's what we do, Jake. . . . That's just what we do." He grunts as we rhythmically pull the pole up hand over hand. It's heavier than I remember, and Gene's knuckles are white with strain. As the last bit of pole comes up out of the blackness, I anticipate the bullrake filled with quahogs. The water starts to boil, churning to white foam.

Lightning flashes! The water explodes, and a giant shark propels itself, teeth first, into the window.

• • •

I shoot up out of bed. My sheets are soaked with sweat. I look out the window and see that the Riptide Diner is still on dry land. No shark either. My clock radio starts beeping. Or maybe it was beeping the whole time? Nope, it reads 5:30 a.m. I slap my hand down on the large brown button, stopping the noise, and grab my jeans off the floor. I try to replay the dream in my head, but already it's dissolving into nothingness. I pull on my high-tops and sniff a few different shirts lying around the floor.

By the time I get downstairs, I'm still feeling messed up and out of sorts as I prepare the diner for the day. I try to count tiles, or count the silverware, or count anything, but by the time I reach seven or eight, my mind spins out again. I have two weeks left to come up with a little more than nine thousand dollars, and I have no idea how I'm gonna do it without Gene. I could go and work for one of the other quahoggers, like he said, but still I'm not going to make the kind of money I need.

"How's Gene?" Robin asks as she hurries from table to table, laying out ketchup bottles and pink packets of sweetener. "I heard what happened. You're a hero, you know."

"He's good. Should be out in another couple of days." I smile weakly, because I know the real hero was Captain.

He saved Gene. I mean, I bandaged him up all right, and kept him warm with my body, and did all that other stuff to help stop the bleeding, but if it wasn't for Captain, Gene would have bled to death right there on the deck of the Hawkline.

"Darcy and I will get the rest," Robin says, taking the tray of silverware from my hands. "Go have some fun." I look over at Darcy and she gives me a thumbs-up.

"We got it, Stretch. Take the day off."

"Thanks," I say, and head upstairs to my room.

When I am back upstairs, two things smash into my brain at the same time.

Captain saved Gene's life. Captain can save me.

That's it. Who else ever gave me three hundred dollars after less than an hour's worth of work? Plus, he knows something about my dad. He has to. *What about the knife?*

I decide to go find Captain again.

I take my bike down to Charon's Dock to see if his boat is still moored there, but it's not and I continue searching.

An hour later I'm walking through the door into Muldoon's Bar. It's only ten thirty in the morning, so I am not really expecting him to be here, but you never know with a guy like him. The bar looks different with all the lights on, less scary in a way. The stools are empty. Most of them are cracked and worn thin at the seams, while some are held together with duct tape.

"We're not open till eleven," a voice calls out from below the bar.

"No, I was . . . I was just looking for somebody," I answer, and head back through the door.

"Wait a minute, kid." I turn around and the bartender gives me a long look. "You Jake?"

"Yes, sir," I say, a little surprised.

"Yeah, I can tell, real tall kid, he said. I got something for you." The bartender is looking between all the liquor bottles on the shelf. "I know I put it somewhere. Aha! Here it is."

"Thanks," I say, confused as he hands me a tightly folded piece of paper.

"Yeah, guy said if you'd come here lookin' for him, I was supposed to give you that. Gave me twenty bucks too. He your dad or something?"

"No! But thanks . . . for this." I hold up the folded paper and head back out onto the street. I find a bench and open the note.

If you want work, meet me at the beach near Kenyon's Bait Shop tomorrow night 10:30 p.m.

There's no name, but I can tell from the handwriting it's Captain. My heart skips a beat because I know I'll probably make some quick cash, but I might get killed. Captain is not what you'd call a safety-first type of guy. I could also end up in jail. But at this point I don't know what's worse: jail or Arizona.

What will my dad think of this? I don't think he wants me working for a guy like Captain, but he should have thought of that before he went missing, leaving us in debt to some stupid loan sharks!

I crumple the paper, stuff it in my pocket, and head down to the water, spending the rest of the morning and most of the afternoon just walking around by the docks near the marina, thinking about Gene, my dad, the beach opening, and Captain's note. I don't know what is right and what is wrong, what is a dream and what is real. *I wish Tommy were back.*

Around four thirty, when I get back to the diner, Darcy is cleaning. I can see her working as I look through the front windows. She moves fast, wiping everything down before placing it back on the table. She's got her headphones on, and she's sort of dancing between the tables. I stand there watching her for a few minutes, until she notices me. She throws her rag down and tromps over to the window and removes her headphones.

"I'm sorry, *sir,* we're closed. You'll have to come back

in the morning," she says through the glass. I just smile and walk around to the back door and head inside. I shuffle into the dining room, plopping down in the first booth with a loud groan.

"All right, what's going on?" Darcy puts down a tray of salt- and pepper shakers, throws the rag over her shoulder, and slides in next to me. I scoot over to give her some room, but not much, and our thighs are touching just slightly. Her leg feels warm.

"Nah, I don't want to talk about it." It sounds pretty weak, probably because I *do* want to talk about it. Darcy can tell.

"Come on, Jake," Darcy says, looking around. "You got to let it out or your brain's going to pop like that guy—what's his name?—Ben."

"Ben Dunn." I laugh.

"Yeah, God knows we don't need another Ben Dunn around here, so tell me what's going on. Is your mom still talking about giving up the diner?"

"She hasn't said anything lately, but I've been avoiding it with her anyway. Here's the thing . . . we owe a lot of money to these guys, and if we don't pay them by the end of the month, they are going to take the diner."

"Oh, my God. I didn't know that. How much do you owe, and to who?"

"Ten grand. To the Mafia . . . I mean, you know, those guys down at the Italian Club."

Darcy's eyes go wide. "That must be why she started in on you about moving to your grandmother's."

"Yeah, I figured out that much. Gene was going to help me. We were going to make the money to pay it off, and with Barrington Beach opening . . . but now that's pretty screwed. I feel like all this stuff's happening to mess me up, like it's all a big test."

"You mean like fate?" Darcy asks.

"I don't know. Yeah, fate, I guess. Like Gene getting hurt just before the beach opens. I mean, why now?"

"Well, sometimes I believe in fate, but only when it makes sense or works out for me. Like the time I went to the movie theater, and that creepy guy followed me to the parking lot, and then, just *then,* my big brother shows up and chases the guy away. *That* was fate. And when I walked in to get some toast, and your mom said she was looking for waitresses, and she hired me right on the spot. That was total fate, because now I have tons of friends and Robin and Trax and Tommy and you. And I feel normal again."

"Well, this fate thing isn't working out too good for me right now." I start playing with the saltshakers, because I'm feeling awkward and I don't know what to do with my hands.

94

"Well, maybe it's just bad luck," Darcy says, eyeing the saltshakers that I keep knocking over. "We just have to work on changing your luck." I'm running my fingers through the salt, creating little pathways across the tray.

Suddenly, and unexpectedly, Darcy puts her hand on mine. I can't tell if she did it to stop my nervous twitching, or if she wants to hold my hand.

Maybe both.

I'm frozen stiff. I can't move my hand, and I don't want to. I force my hand to relax, and her slender hand softens and settles onto mine.

I can feel my ears turning red. Not because I'm embarrassed, but because I'm happy. No one's saying anything; we're just sitting together in the booth. I'm not looking at her, just staring out the front windows, and when my eyes drift down, I can see our reflection. Darcy's looking too. She notices and smiles at me. It's hard to see, but her eyes sparkle. I am afraid to look at her even though she's only a foot away, and it feels like there is a fire burning between our hands.

In the glass, I see Robin walking in from the kitchen, carrying aprons. I pull my hand away quickly.

"Oh, sorry, sorry. I didn't know you guys were in here . . . *together.*" Robin pretends to hide behind the aprons.

Darcy gets up and immediately starts cleaning the

backs of the chairs at the next table. "We weren't together."

"She's right. We weren't together." I scramble out of the booth, knocking all the saltshakers to the floor. I don't know why I'm saying this because we *were* together for a minute or two, and besides, I like Darcy.

Now there it is.

I said it to myself and I keep saying it in my head. *I like Darcy.*

"I am glad you're not together. I've been waiting for you to *not* be together all summer." Robin piles the aprons into the hamper near the kitchen and disappears through the double doors. I look over at Darcy, and we both start laughing out loud just as my mom comes in and wrecks it all.

11

THREE TREE ISLAND

Wednesday morning, August 18

I know that I am going to be working with Captain again tonight, so when Tommy calls to see if I want to go skating, I think it might be a good chance to forget everything and blow off some steam.

"What's up?" I say as Tommy slips through his front door, bringing his finger to his lips. I follow him down his steps and to the street. I motion to the window where his little sister, Annie, is staring hard and swishing one index finger across the other like she's peeling a carrot. Tommy glares back and flinches at her with his balled up fist until she disappears and the shade settles back into place.

"Is she going to rat you out?" I ask, dropping my skateboard to the pavement.

"Nah. She's all right. They're all going down to the church today, some volunteer crap." Tommy is about to put his skateboard down, then he looks at me. "But if you want to go with them, it should be *real* fun. I know how much you like to work."

"Let me see, skating with you . . . or . . . working all day at the church with your five brothers and sisters." I walk back toward his door.

"Come on, ya chowderhead." Tommy punches me hard in the shoulder with his knuckle and takes off down the street.

For the next couple hours we don't talk much. We're just glad to be out skating around and practicing tricks. Tommy's getting pretty good, and right now I suck. *Unco on land, unco on wheels.* I ollie up and try to grind across the curb on Water Street and fall headfirst into a parked car. Some people start staring, so we quickly cut over to Main Street and head north.

"Cherry Cokes at Deluca's! I'm buying," I say as we wind down the street.

"Of course you're buyin'. What do you have, like six jobs now?"

We both get Cokes and continue to roll through town, playing follow the leader. Tommy takes a right on Kelly

Street and heads down toward the Palmer River. I get this buzzy, hot feeling because the Italian-American Club is at the end of Kelly Street, and that's where those loan sharks hang out.

"Where you going?" I kick my board to a stop about halfway down the street.

"Found something the other day. Come on."

I follow Tommy toward the eelgrass at the end of Kelly, staring at the Italian-American Club on the right side of the street. It's a one-story cinder-block building painted puke brown, with a big sign that's exactly like the emblem that those guys who came into the diner had on the back of their jackets. There are eight cars and trucks in the lot, and a big sign over the windowless door that says MEMBERS ONLY. I want to take a wrecking ball to the place. I see it exploding in my head, bodies flying through the air and landing with a sucking wet thud in the marsh.

"Over here." Tommy is darting through the eelgrass toward the beach. We used to come down here when we were little and collect old bottles and pottery 'cause it used to be the town dump. Tommy is sitting in an old rowboat half-filled with water, tied to a cinder block. The line is frayed, and it looks like no one has rowed this boat in fifteen years.

There's a bailing scoop made from a cut laundry-detergent bottle floating in the stern. Tommy holds it up so I can see the bleached-out TIDE label printed on the side.

"Nice name for a bailer." I laugh.

Tommy motions with his hands. "The tide runs into the boat . . . and the tide runs out of the boat."

"Think it floats?"

Tommy steals a glance out into the Palmer River. "Only one way to find out. Be right back." He jumps out of the boat and jogs back up the street. I grab the bailer and start getting the water out. Paint peels right off the deck with every scoop. I look up, and Tommy is lifting a set of oars from the back of a red pickup truck parked in the driveway of the Italian-American Club. He's running with the oars, making twisted, serpentine movements through the marsh. Tommy's always half stealing something. I mean, he borrows stuff he figures people don't need, and then he brings it back later. I wonder if Tommy knows about the Law of Finds.

"It's looking good now." Tommy pants as he approaches and sees the nearly dry rowboat. He throws the oars in, and we both put our skateboards behind a nearby hedge because we don't want anyone *borrowing* them.

Pushing the heavy, waterlogged boat over the shell-covered beach, I can see traces of oil oozing from the sand. It mixes with the water and creates colorful, swirling rainbows.

We cast off for Three Tree Island, which is a small, marshy island in the middle of the Palmer River. It has a sandy beach on one side, a rocky shoreline on the other, and three pathetic-looking trees in the middle. It used to have more trees, and a different name, but some kids were partying out there, and they had a huge fire going and they burned down almost the entire island. *Idiots.*

The boat seems to float, but it definitely requires two people to operate. One of us has to bail continuously while the other rows. I notice that every time Tommy pulls on the oars, his feet push the old plywood bottom down, and more water rushes into the boat.

"Step on these. You're sinking us." I say, pointing to the oak braces that hold the tub together. Three Tree Island is within a few hundred yards, so I figure we'll make it there, but if we don't, we can just swim it. God knows how we'll get back.

To this point we are still dry, so I offer to row for a while. Tommy's enjoying the ride, leaning back on the stern and letting his hands drag through the water.

I rest the oars on my lap and look back toward Warren. "Can I tell you something?"

Tommy sits up on his elbows. "What?"

I tell Tommy everything; the loan sharks, the money, how Gene was going to help me, the beach opening, Captain, the knife . . . *everything*. The only thing I don't tell him is how I think this is all a test from my dad. He'd probably think I've lost it completely.

"So you're going to work for a pirate? That's awesome! Can I come?"

"No, you idiot. Captain would slice my throat for even telling you." I say this as kind of a joke, but there may be some truth to it.

"You think you'll make enough to pay them off?" Tommy glances back at the Italian-American Club on the shoreline.

"I hope so."

"I'll figure out a way to help. I don't want you moving away."

"Thanks," I say.

"I mean, where else am I gonna get free milk and donuts every morning?"

"You're such a jackass." I grab one of the oars and flick it hard on the water, sending spray all over him. Tommy grabs the other and does the same, and soon we're both soaked from the volley of water.

Ten minutes later we hit bottom at the southern point of Three Tree Island. Tommy and I pull the boat onshore and tie the frayed rope around a barnacle-covered rock. People have definitely been out here. There's a fire pit, and hundreds of beer cans and bottles litter the beach. Tommy's already picking the cans up and tossing them into one of the onion bags also found onshore.

"What are you going to do with those?" I ask, sitting down on an old log by the fire pit.

"They're worth five cents apiece over the border in Massachusetts. It's like picking up nickels," Tommy says, setting one bag into the boat and grabbing another. "Plus, this beach looks like a freakin' dump."

"Give me one of those bags."

Pretty soon we've got five onion bags filled with cans, two bags of bottles, and one bag of trash all piled up in the rowboat.

"It's looking good now." Tommy surveys the beach with a broad grin.

I plop myself down in the sand and take off my wet sneakers and shirt, setting them out to dry. I close my eyes and feel the warm sun on my face. I'm feeling like a kid again. I'm feeling like I did last summer when things were easy, before my dad disappeared, before I turned into a freaky tall Unco. Before my world started falling apart. *Let it go. Just let it go for right now. Let it go until tonight, until I meet up with Captain.*

I hear Tommy marching off into the eelgrass, but I keep my eyes closed and lie still in the sand, waiting for that easy feeling to drift back into my body.

Tommy comes back to the fire pit with a rusty iron pot that looks like it belonged to a witch, a piece of angle iron that must have come off a sunken boat, and a pair of broken and twisted eyeglasses.

"Time to make a fire," Tommy says, dropping everything at my feet.

"I thought your matches got soaked."

"They did." Tommy starts gathering some dried seaweed and crumbling it up into a small pile. I'm watching closely now as he moves the one remaining lens of the eyeglasses around, trying to find the best angle.

"Is that going to work?"

"I don't know. I guess a magnifying glass would be better, or binoculars . . ."

"Or dry matches?"

"Those too."

Tommy's face is inches from the ground, and beads of sweat are gathering on his forehead as he concentrates on the pinpoint of light. Tommy is the thriftiest guy I know. He's always finding ways to reuse stuff that most people would just throw away. I guess part of that comes from having two older brothers. By the time he gets their hand-me-down stuff, he's got to find a way to fix it up and make it last all summer. The sneakers he's wearing now have new soles glued on that he cut from old tires he found. Sometimes he'll get caught picking through people's garbage, so a ton of kids at school call him Trashman Tommy. He's the best recycler you ever saw.

"Grab some small sticks, quick." Tommy's legs are twitching as a whisper of smoke begins to curl from the seaweed. I pick up some dried eelgrass and lay it in his outstretched hand. Tommy blows softly on the pile, and it sparks to life like magic. He cups his hand around the precious flame and arranges a bunch of the eelgrass sticks in a tepee around it. The sticks catch quickly. Tommy adds more fuel, and suddenly there is a beautiful, dancing orange flame.

"I MAKE FIRE!" Tommy is stomping around and beating his chest like a caveman. He puts the broken glasses on his face and dances, throwing both arms in the air. I'm staring at the fire, laughing my butt off because I am just so amazed he did it.

Tommy picks up the witches' pot and hands it to me, speaking like a caveman. "I made fire. *You* make lunch, oooh, ooh."

"All right, all right." I grab the pot and take it down to the edge of the water. I lift a handful of wet sand into the pot and begin scraping its rusty insides until the original color of the metal comes back. It looks good enough to cook in. I fill the pot with salt water and add rockweed for flavor, then carry the pot back and rest it on the metal grate that Tommy set up with the angle iron.

"You gonna feed me rockweed?" Tommy asks, staring into the pot.

"Sit tight, relax, watch, and learn," I say in a cocky tone.

The fire is going really good, and pretty soon the water on the outside of the pot begins to sizzle.

Stripping off my shorts, I walk into the Palmer River up to my chest, feeling with my feet for quahogs. The silky mud slides through my toes as I search. It's not long before I find a nice little patch of quahogs, and I'm dunking under and pulling out one quahog after another, sometimes two at time. I forget to bring a bag or bucket or something to put them in, so I just stuff them into my underwear.

I must look pretty whacky, walking out of the river with twenty-seven quahogs stretching my underwear to the limit. I feel good, like I have accomplished something, just like Tommy did with the fire.

"I hope you're not expecting me to eat those." Tommy crinkles his nose, and his upper lip on one side is quivering dramatically as I start dropping them into the pot.

"Best you've ever tasted." I laugh and grab the

pocketknife out of my shorts. "Now I'm going to get some blue crabs."

"You putting those in your underwear too?"

"No, yours."

I find a straight stick and quickly shave the end into a point as I walk around toward the north side of the island, where there is some shade and I can see through the water better.

I'm real quiet, ready to stab crabs. They're very quick if they sense you and can swim away with their legs. I'm crouching now and see one hanging out just behind a rock. *Bam!* I get one and then two and three and four.

The pot is boiling now, and the crabs are still fighting back with their blue pinchers. We watch them all turn red in a flash as we drop them into the water.

Fifteen minutes later we're both eating like animals. Tommy's a raccoon, crouching down at the water's edge, using a small rock to crack the claws.

"We should just live out here, you know?" I suggest.

Tommy looks up at me, with pieces of white crabmeat all around his mouth. "What, out here on the Palmer River?"

"Yeah. Here, or Prudence Island, anywhere."

Tommy drops a claw into the sand. "You don't think you can get the money to save the diner, do you?"

"Come on, let's start heading back," I say, moving toward the rowboat, avoiding his question. Tommy washes off his hands and follows me.

"That's a real question . . . isn't it? It hurts like a real question?"

"Too real. You just ruined the day," I say, totally bummed out now.

"What can I do to help?" Tommy asks, concerned.

"You have any way to make nine grand real quick?" I ask sarcastically.

"Bottles and cans, Jake. You know how much money we're gonna make for returning this stuff?" he says, all serious.

"No, how much?"

"I'll bet there's fifteen, maybe twenty, bucks' worth of cans and another five worth of bottles," he says, all proud. "The other trash isn't worth anything."

"That's great, Tommy. Now we just need to fill another two thousand bags of cans. That sounds like a perfect idea." I laugh as I push the boat back out into the water.

The river is flat calm this afternoon, and I think we are going to be okay in this overloaded rowboat, until I see that snot, Vinny Vile, racing around in his Boston Whaler. I start to row, keeping one eye on Vinny's boat. Now I'm sure that he is veering toward us.

"He's spotted us, Tommy."

"Who?" Tommy asks, arranging some of the leftover quahogs on the bottom of the boat.

"Vinny." I nod over to the Whaler as it starts to pick up speed. I look back at Tommy, and he looks like he's going to blow a gasket.

"Don't worry, Tommy, they're not going to do anything," I say, standing up in the middle of the rowboat, using the bags of trash for balance.

"He's got that chooch Jim Allen with him," Tommy says.

I can hear them laughing as they approach. Vile's boat comes to an idle, and the motor shakes like it's trying to release itself from the stern.

"Jim, look, it's Trashman and Unco." Vile's words spew from his mouth like grease from a grease gun. Neither of us says anything. "You two Boy Scouts trying to get a merit badge?"

"Girl Scouts," the chooch says, and they both start laughing out loud. The motor revs; Vinny jams it into gear and starts circling us, making a big wake. The trash starts knocking back and forth, and our boat is leaking badly.

A quahog shatters on the bow of their boat, and pieces of shell fly like shrapnel. I look over, and Tommy is standing up with two more quahogs and taking aim at the guys. One zings past Jim's head as he ducks, and Vinny cuts the wheel hard, guns the engine, and flees from Tommy's onslaught.

The Whaler is halfway up the river, and Tommy is still slinging quahogs at them.

"They're gone, Tommy! They're gone." But Tommy is still throwing quahogs at the fleeing boat and biting his lip. When the last quahog splashes into the water, Tommy sits down. His fists are clenched and drumming on his thighs. "Jesus, Tommy, what the hell was that? You could have killed one of those guys."

"I wanted to. They're complete scumbags, and they would have deserved it."

"I can't blame you there. But I've never seen you like that. You were possessed, man," I say, straightening the bags.

"Let's just get home. I don't want those jerks coming back."

"Yeah." I pull on the oars. "We'd have to start throwing bottles at them, and they're worth five cents apiece."

Tommy is still pissed but he starts sputtering, and then he laughs and begins to look like himself again. We get to shore and decide to leave the bottles and cans in the boat for now. Maybe we'll come back another day and sell them. We quietly place the oars back in the truck that is still parked at the Italian-American Club, and throw the trash in the Dumpster behind the building near the bocce courts.

As we come back around the corner, I grab Tommy and shove him down behind a black four-door sedan.

"What the hell?" Tommy complains.

"Shhhh." I point to the green-and-tan Chevy Blazer pulling up to the front of the Italian-American Club. Tommy sees the DEM logo on the side of the truck and quickly understands.

As we peek through the dusty windows of the sedan, the Blazer comes to a stop, and who gets out but that guy Delvecchio. I can see huge sweat stains on his uniform as he cautiously opens the back of the Blazer.

"What do you think he's doing? You think he's going to bust the guys at the Italian Club?" Tommy asks in a hushed whisper.

"I don't know." I continue to watch, waiting for Delvecchio to pull out a shotgun or a bazooka or something. I can see his skinny blond-haired partner twitching in the front seat. Delvecchio definitely pulls something out of the back of the Blazer, but from where we are, I can't see what it is until he gets to the door.

"What's he doing bringing quahogs to the Italian Club?" Tommy asks.

"I'm not sure." I watch as a big guy with the name CAZZO embroidered on his black satin jacket sticks his fat head and chest out of the half-opened door. I immediately recognize him from the diner, and my heart races. Delvecchio hands him two onion bags filled with littlenecks, and they exchange nods. I can't hear what they're saying, but Delvecchio gives him a wave, and Tommy and I both duck down as he turns back toward his truck. We stay like that until we see the Blazer pull out of the parking lot.

"What's up with *that*?" Tommy asks as we head back to the marsh to collect our skateboards.

"That clam cop was the one who came into the Riptide and started busting chops last week."

"What's he running, a quahog delivery service part-time?"

"Who knows? Maybe he owes Vito ten grand too." I say this, knowing it's probably something a whole lot worse. "Come on, let's get out of here."

"Good idea," Tommy says, brushing off his skateboard.

"So really, what did Vinny and Jim do to you to make you want to kill them?" I ask Tommy as we head back up Kelly Street.

"You don't want to know."

"What?" I ask, coming to a stop. "I told you about all the crazy stuff going on with me."

Tommy kicks his skateboard up and walks over to me. "They locked me in a Dumpster."

"They *what?*"

"Those bastards locked me in the Dumpster at school. You know the one behind the cafeteria near the bike racks? It was full of grease and all kinds of nasty stuff, and I threw up all over myself. By the time the janitor opened it up, there was a crowd of people standing around and laughing at me, and I just ran."

"God, if I had known, I would have been chucking chowders at them too."

"Look, it doesn't matter. What matters is that we save the diner." He's poking me in the ribs now, and I can see tears welling up in his eyes. "We have to save that diner, because if you move away and leave me here alone with those jerks, I *will* kill them."

I don't know what to say.

Tommy quickly wipes his eyes and takes off.

Great. Yet another reason I have to go out in the middle of the night and work for a pirate and risk my life to pay off some Mafia loan sharks so that I can keep living in a tiny apartment above the diner—so Tommy doesn't kill Vinny Vile and Jim Allen and go off to prison.

Thanks, Dad. This is getting better all the time.

12

A PIRATE'S LIFE FOR ME

Wednesday night, August 18

At a little past ten I walk down to Kenyon's Bait Shop and take the wooden stairs down to the small sandy beach. It's pitch-dark, with no moon; it even feels like a night for pirates. I wonder what we're going to "salvage" tonight. A splinter from the railing rips into my finger as I get to the last step. *Definitely a sign. Turn back. Go home. Forget the money and the diner and just suck it up and move to Arizona.*

I can't see, so I just leave the splinter lodged in my hand and sit down in the sand at the edge of the water to wait.

The water glistens from the reflected lights of the houses across the river in Barrington. I begin to think about Darcy and her jet-black hair, and her blue eyes that sparkle every time she makes a joke. I wonder about her arm, and I understand why she hides it. Kids are mean. Guys like Vinny Vile and Jim Allen are too damn stupid to know how much they hurt people.

Ten minutes later I can hear Captain's engines rumble in the distance, like growling bears biting through the darkness. The growl turns to a churning scream as he trims the engines up and the hull of the boat crunches onto the shell-covered beach.

I rise from the sand, grab the bow rail, and swing my leg on board as we silently back away from the beach without speaking a word. It's creepy and exciting and I know there's no turning back.

"Take the wheel," Captain demands, and I do what he says, using the lights of the houses onshore to guide me out of the mouth of the river.

"I can't see anything."

"That's the idea." Captain pulls out a rolled-up black cloth. He grabs the wheel and uses his hip to shove me aside as he pulls the cloth over and snaps it around the console, instantly blacking out the light coming from the instrument panel. He takes one last look around at the lights on land, and then dips his head underneath the shroud.

Holy crap, he's going to steer this boat using only instruments. I've heard of guys having to do that in a thick fog, or in a snowstorm, but I've never actually seen it.

We're moving past Barrington Beach, and my mind wanders to the opening next week. I'm wondering if Captain is going to work the beach when it opens. The boat slows to a crawl, and suddenly I'm thinking that Captain is going to work the beach right now. He doesn't have any bullrakes or poles or any other quahogging equipment on board, so I'm not sure. He does have a large davit anchored to the deck and the gunwale, like the kind Gene uses to haul lobster traps. I think we're going to steal lobster traps, and I'm starting to break out in a cold sweat. In Maine, lobstermen will shoot you dead for stealing traps.

"Get the grappling hook out of the anchor well." Captain shoots his instructions from underneath the shroud. "When I give you the signal, lower it over the starboard side till it hits bottom."

I follow his instructions, but I wish Captain would clue me in. *Are we salvaging again? What's down there?* At least on Gene's boat, I know what the drill is.

The grappling hook clangs onto something, and the rope jerks and nearly pulls me overboard. Captain grabs the rope from my hand and threads it through the pulley at the end of the davit. Looping the rope around a hydraulic winch near the base, he pulls a lever and the rope goes taut.

"What are we pulling up?" I whisper.

"You'll see." Captain's eyes stay fixed as the rope snakes into the boat.

He reaches over and shuts down the winch as a rusty metal cage breaks the surface of the water. He swings it into the boat and brings it down quietly on the rubber mats.

"What is that? It looks like a bullrake built for giants."

"You ever see anything that catches ten thousand quahogs in less than three hours?"

"No," I answer.

"Well, now you have," he says with a proud smirk on his face. "Easiest money you'll ever make, kid. Just you wait and see. Keep your mouth shut, work hard, and at the end of the week you'll be flush with cash," Captain says as he nervously adjusts the top button on his shirt.

I stare at him as he dips beneath the black shroud and leans into the throttle, pointing the boat toward the Providence River.

Minutes later the engines wind down, and I am feeling like a real pirate now. Here we are in the polluted Providence River, about to dredge the bottom for quahogs. This is even crazier than salvaging engines in the middle of a hurricane.

Three hours, flush with cash. Three hours, flush with cash. That's what I keep telling myself.

13

NIGHT DREDGING

Friday night, August 20

The night shadows seem like ghosts behind each wave. Random noises pierce the air. A barbecue grill being closed, a car door slamming shut; it's all crystal clear as the sounds travel across the Providence River from the eastern shore. Each time I hear a noise I don't recognize, I'm sure it's the clam cops, and it seems like they're right on top of us.

It's the third night in a row I've been out here with Captain, dredging the bottom of the Providence River for quahogs. Captain was right; I've never seen anything like it. We caught about ten thousand quahogs in a little over two hours both nights. Ten thousand! I put two hundred and fifty in each bag, and the secret storage compartment underneath the deck only holds forty bags, so when it's full, we leave, no matter what.

Each night we take the bags and string them up far out in the ocean so the quahogs can clean themselves; that way, no one gets sick when they eat them. Captain's got this whole operation figured out pretty good. I'm still waiting to get paid. The quahogs have to sit in clean water for two weeks before we can sell them, so I probably won't get paid for a while. I just hope nothing gets messed up before I get my money. Last night, I told him I needed to get paid by the end of the month, and he didn't hear me, or he acted like he didn't hear me because he didn't say anything. Most of the time he doesn't talk at all. I just get picked up at Kenyon's Dock every night around ten, come out here, do my job till my fingers are raw, and get dropped off around one a.m. Then I sleep until five a.m., set up the diner, and go back to bed for the rest of the day. Now I know why Captain is so pale — I haven't seen the sun in days.

Tonight, we haven't been out here very long, and I've already got thirty-two bags in the well. I push the button on my digital watch and the blue-green face lights up, but before I can read the time, Captain has my wrist in a death grip. He twists it hard, and with a swipe of his thick index finger, breaks the plastic clasp of my watch.

"What are you, stupid or something, kid?" He grunts through clenched teeth, waving the watch in front of my face. "You might as well be shooting flares into the sky.

You think they're not out here? You think they're not looking for us?" I think he's going to throw my watch overboard. Instead he tosses it into the small cabin below the console. "*Never* bring that out on the water again. Not even in your pocket, you understand?"

I'm shaking all over, and my wrist stings where he grabbed me. "Got it, Cap." I face the deck with my head down.

"Good," he says, wiping white spit from the sides of his mouth.

The boat is moving in a wide arc, and Captain grabs the wheel, checks his bearings, and gets us back on course. I'm still shaking from the encounter, and Captain looks back and says with a grin, "If you have to know, it's eleven thirty-five."

"That's cool." I exhale. I didn't even realize I was holding my breath. "Is this the last haul?" I ask, my voice cracking.

"Could be. I'm looking for my hot spot. It's right up ahead. The quahogs are all jammed up against one another, like little bowling pins ready for us to strike. You'll hear it soon."

Suddenly the boat shudders and I'm thrown off balance.

"Is this it?" I ask.

Captain throws his muscular arm over my shoulder and pulls me in close.

"Hear the engines straining? See the post? See how it's twitching?" He grabs my hand and pins it down on the gunwale. "You feel that? We're stuffing that dredge like a Thanksgiving turkey." He slaps me on the back, and I can tell this will be the last haul of the night.

"I can feel it."

"Good! Now don't tell me I never taught you nothing." Captain ducks back under the shroud and starts muttering to himself.

After a couple minutes, the engines idle. Captain comes out and scans the horizon in all directions.

"They out here?" I ask, about the cops.

"They're always out here." He pulls the lever, and the winch comes alive as the rope snakes its way onto the deck. "When this haul comes on board, sort everything fast, and get the quahogs below deck."

"Got it, Cap."

"Get caught with this stuff on board and we're screwed."

The dredge begins to rise from the bottom of the river, and Captain's right leg is jumping up and down, like a little kid waiting to get on the bumper cars at Rocky Point amusement park. As it breaks the surface, the dredge looks like the open mouth of a shark, dripping with water and mud and quahogs spilling out, its metal teeth glinting from the lights of the city. The rake drops to the deck and lands with a dull thud on the rubber mats.

"Okay, get her open, quick," he whispers sharply.

I open the stainless-steel clips at the back of the dredge, and the quahogs dump into a pile. "Nice haul."

"That should do it." Captain nods at the pile and turns his attention back to the empty dredge and dumps it over the side.

I wash the quahogs with a stream of pressurized water from the flexible hose connected to the water pump. The boat lurches forward as I drop to my knees and begin to count quahogs into a half-bushel basket. I do it by feel in the dark, three in my right hand and two in my left. When I get to two hundred and fifty, I dump them into the mesh bag, close it, and get it below deck as quickly as possible. My knees ache and my back cramps only minutes into the work.

Thirty minutes later, I snap the metal clip on the fortieth bag and wedge it into the storage compartment and lock it shut.

"Are you sure you want me to dump this?" I say, nodding at the rest of the uncounted quahogs on deck.

"We got forty bags below deck?"

"Yeah, it's all there." I hand Captain the small key.

"Dump the rest."

This part is torture. It's like throwing money out the window, and I need every dime right now. I have to force myself not to count as I toss shovelfuls of quahogs over the side of the moving boat. When that's done, I spray the decks and place fishing rods in the pole holder so we look like two guys going out to fish on Block Island.

Captain stops the boat just beyond Beavertail Point, leaving the helm as the boat sits adrift in the moving swells. I know what's next.

"Turn around."

I turn and face the bow as the black cloth comes over my eyes, blocking out all light. Captain cinches it behind my head and pulls on the knot, making sure it's secure. The thing is so tight, my eyeballs are pressing into my skull. He's so freaking paranoid he even ties my hands behind the leaning post, so I can't take the blindfold off.

"You don't have to do this," I say to him.

"The less you know, the better. I'm just keeping you innocent. If someone steals my stuff, I don't want to have to think it was you."

The boat rolls to the south and slams the waves between each swell as my insides begin jumping around. I bend my knees to absorb the shock, but with every unseen wave I feel like I'm in a car accident that won't end. Most people would be puking their brains out, but I never get sick. I've been in a boat since forever.

"You all right?" Captain shouts above the noise of the engines and the pounding hull.

"I'm still not used to it," I scream. "It's my hands. I need my hands to brace myself."

"Hang on, we're almost there."

"Where? Where are we going?"

"Places, kid, places. We're going places." I can hear him laughing as he says these words.

"Ahh, come on," I urge him further.

"If I told you, I'd have to kill ya."

The boat stops and the engines idle down. Captain removes my blindfold and releases my arms from the straps. I look around and see the large red cylinder, bobbing twenty feet from the bow. It's amazing how he finds this little red dot in the middle of the ocean.

"Get the bowline and tie it off the red can."

"I got it. I know." It's my third night out here. I want him to know I'm not stupid.

I secure us to the can, unlock the storage compartment, and start getting the bags of quahogs ready to be clipped onto the line that stretches to the anchor at the bottom of this ledge.

"Hold on with those." I turn around and Captain is

hauling in a line with full bags already on it. "We're selling out tonight."

"Those are the clean ones?" I ask. "They look almost white."

"Would you believe the New Yorkers pay even more for these?" Captain laughs as he unclips the first bag and hands it to me. "Put that on the port side, and don't mix them up."

Fifteen minutes later we've got forty bags of clean quahogs in the locked storage compartment, and we've secured the other forty on the line.

"Where are we selling out?" I ask.

"Turn around." I see Captain reaching for the blindfold.

Oh, crap.

14

THE BLUE KITTEN

Friday night, August 20

The engines throttle down, and Captain lets me loose.
My wrists are raw, and I rub them gingerly while
waiting for my eyes to adjust to the light. I've been
to Block Island a couple times before, but I don't
remember this harbor. It may be the thick fog blanket-
ing the small inlet, changing the look of the place. A
few drunken shouts echo off the water as our boat slides
toward a long, narrow dock with a row of lobster boats
tied to it.

As I look down the fleet of boats, I can see a blue-
and-white rack of lights mounted to the top of a DEM
boat at the far end. I grab the wheel and yank it hard to
the port side. The boat swings in behind the last lobster
boat. Captain throttles back.

"What the hell are you doing?" His eyes are wide with rage. I take a step back, pointing to the DEM boat over my shoulder. He understands and throws the boat in reverse, slowing us down. We drift in behind the lobster boat. I tie us off. Captain reaches beneath the console and pulls out two long magnetic strips that have different registration numbers. He slaps them over the current numbers on either side of the bow.

This guy is the James Bond of quahogging.

Next he pulls out the fishing gear and hands it to me. "Start rigging up some leaders and look busy. I'm going to duck up the street till this cowboy leaves."

"How do you know he's going to leave?"

"Believe me, he'll leave. This isn't a place a clam cop would want to hang around too long."

"And you want me to start fishing?"

"Fish. Don't fish. I don't give a crap. Just look like you're doing something." Captain shoots a sickening smile at me before he scrambles across the lobster boat and down the dock. I watch as he disappears into the shadows.

For the next ten minutes, I am scanning the dock and pretending to fish. There's a rock song pumping through some small, rusty speakers attached to the pylons. At the end of the dock there is a gray-shingled wharf house. The only light in the harbor is coming from a blue neon cat mounted to the sagging roof. The cat's tail cycles through a series of poses that make it look like it's moving to the beat of the music. It must be closing time because suddenly ten guys shuffle out the front door and start off in different directions along the waterfront. The last guy out the door starts slowly down the dock. He's counting money. As he gets closer, I can hear him. I duck down low and peer between the ropes.

"Forty-three, forty-four, forty-five hundred." He stops, and I can just make out his satisfied grin as he folds the wad and stuffs it in his shirt pocket. He's not wearing a uniform, but I can see from his size and that bald head that it's Delvecchio. *Of course.*

I'm holding my breath as he climbs aboard the DEM boat, just thirty feet from me. As the boat pulls away, his lights illuminate the small harbor in a pulse of blue and white. Delvecchio pegs the engine full bore, and the boat shoots out into open sea like a dart. I can finally breathe, letting the fishing pole drop to the deck with a loud rattle.

"All right, let's go," Captain says in my ear, and I nearly jump right out of my skin.

"What'd you sneak up on me like that for? I almost crapped myself." I watch Captain start the engines, and I untie the lines in a hurry. He swings the boat around to the empty spot where Delvecchio just left.

"Where we going?" I ask.

"The Blue Kitten." Captain nods toward the wharf house. "Leave everything here."

I secure the boat and start to climb onto the dock when Captain grabs my shoulder, spinning me around, and looks me straight in the eye. The beads of sweat on his upper lip dance up and down as he says, "You watch yourself in there, you hear me? This place isn't Disneyland. You got that knife I gave you?"

"What?" I get a queasy feeling in my stomach as he turns to the upper hatch, opens it, and removes a gun, sticking it beneath his shirt.

"The knife, you got it?" Captain is almost whispering as he shoots a look toward the door.

"My dad's knife? Yeah, I got it," I say, pulling the knife from my pocket and handing it to him. *It's now or never.* "Do you know my dad?"

"Look, kid, your dad's gone. He gave me this and I wanted you to have it. That's it," he says abruptly.

"So you *do* know him. Tell me where he is."

"Bottom of the ocean," Captain says, looking away.

My body is shaking. I can feel the blood pounding in my temples. "I don't believe it," I say. "Did you see him die?"

"No. No, I read it in the papers just like everyone else." Captain brushes me off. "No more questions. Now put that knife away."

"But—"

"Enough!" Captain grunts. "Follow me and do what I say. Catching quahogs is easy; selling them can be trouble. This shouldn't take long if things go well, but we can't sit out here chatting like a couple of tourists." Captain rubs his thigh as he limps down the dock toward the building.

Now I'm more confused than ever.

Sitting on a wooden stool, just inside the door, is a muscular guy with snake tattoos covering his arms like sleeves. He's reading the paper with a small, silver flashlight clenched between his teeth. He looks up at Captain and nods his head slightly, pulling the dark velvet curtain back and revealing the inside of the bar. Light pours through the opening as he studies my face.

"Listen, buddy, you can't bring the kid in here," the guy says, stopping me in my tracks with his palm on my chest.

"I can just wait outside," I quickly offer.

Captain slowly turns around and faces the guy, his eyes tightening into lasers. He looks at the guy's hand, which is still pressed up against my chest, then gradually brings his stare to the guy's face and holds it there. It's like a showdown, and I don't know which one of them is going to slug the other, or pull out a gun, or what. I'm afraid.

The bouncer's meaty hand cautiously comes away from my chest and snaps open the newspaper again, then sticks the flashlight back into his mouth. Captain turns and heads into the bar, and I follow him. I try to act cool, but I trip over the stool and stumble into him. *I must be on land.*

Luckily, Captain ignores my shove, focusing on the back of the bar, where two guys are coming out from behind a velvet curtain like the one we just walked through. They are holding another guy up by the arms between them. He looks like a real swamper fisherman: black rubber boots, flannel shirt, dark tanned face with lots of stubble. His legs are slack and dragging behind him, his head wobbling between his shoulders like a broken doll. At first I'm thinking he's just drunk, but then I notice the blood smeared across his nose and cheek, and the dark stain on his jeans. *He's pissed his pants.* I reach into my pocket and check for my knife again.

We both watch as they drag him past us, out the front door. The curtain in the back of the bar is thrown open again, and out walks one of the largest men I have ever seen. I don't mean fat, although he doesn't look like he skips any meals. I mean big, like polar-bear big. He has thin, sandy-blond hair raked across his tanned forehead and eyes that sparkle like blue chips of ice in the bright light of the bar. His sweat-stained tropical shirt is unbuttoned to his belly, revealing a large gold anchor hanging from a chain around his neck.

"George Hassard!" the guy says, slapping a hairy arm on Captain. "How's it hangin'?"

George Hassard? Hassard? I look at Captain and my mouth falls open. I can't believe it. Gene's brother or cousin or whatever; this guy I've been working for is somehow related to Gene. *That's how he knows my dad.* Captain's eyes dart over to me for an instant.

"King." He nods cautiously at the man and hands him a key, the same key I used to lock the storage compartment that holds the quahogs we pulled off the stringer. King juggles the key in his hand for a second, and suddenly there is a loud scream followed by a splash that brings a smile to his face, revealing several gold fillings.

"I have a terrible feeling they just threw that guy off the dock, and he was in no shape to swim anywhere. Good thing it's low tide." King laughs. "The little bastard thought he could steal from me." King waves a dismissive hand. "What can I get you? Jamaican coffee? Nick! Two Jamaican coffees." King barks over his shoulder at the bartender, without waiting for Captain's answer. "And get the kid whatever he wants." King studies me for a second before looking at Captain. "What, are you coaching basketball now, George?"

"He's tall, but he works hard and keeps his mouth shut." Captain gives me a hard stare.

Then King looks at me and says, "Get yourself a burger or something, on me, and I'll put in a good word for you with the Celtics." He laughs heartily and puts one arm around George, leading him to a small table in the back corner.

I watch as King tosses the key over to the corner of the bar. A thin, bearded man with dark circles under his eyes steps out of the shadows just in time to catch it.

"Unload 'em fast," King barks at him. The skinny guy nods and slips out the front door like an eel.

Looking around, I notice this isn't just a regular bar like Muldoon's in Warren. There is a small circular stage a few feet high with a chrome pole in the center that's bolted to the ceiling. I've heard about places like this. I can't believe I am actually in one. Tommy would flip out if he knew I was in a strip club! I walk over to the bar, and before I am halfway there, the bartender, Nick, presses both hands down on the bar and says, "Kitchen's closed."

I look over at Captain and he is already behind me, staring hard at this guy Nick. "Look, just get the kid a burger or something. He's starving."

"I said the kitchen's closed." Nick sneers and resumes polishing the beer taps with his rag.

King steps between Captain and the bar and says, "I'll take care of this. Nick's new here." King reaches into his pocket and pulls out a round metal token about the size of a quarter, snapping it down on the bar in front of Nick.

Nick picks it up nervously. "What's this?" He studies the token. "What *is* this?"

King pauses and then says, "That's your first-strike token."

"What am I supposed to do with it?" Nick asks.

"Save 'em up and see what happens when you get three." King heads back to his table and Captain follows.

Nick continues staring at King as he walks away and asks, "What'd ya say you wanted, kid?"

"A burger."

"No problem." Nick draws it out between clenched teeth as he gives King and Captain one last look. "You want fries with that?"

"Sure."

I pull out one of the heavy oak stools and sit down. There is a long mirror behind the bar, and I notice how tired I look. My slouch is getting worse too. I try to straighten up, but it just shoots pain through my lower back. Bending over the side of that boat and lifting those bags from the water really did me in. I give in to the pain and rest my head on my arm, hoping to get a little sleep before the food comes. My eyes slowly close and I am gone.

"You okay, honey?" A raspy voice pulls me from sleep.

I look up and feel drool sliding down the side of my face. I wipe my mouth of spit, and coming out of my fog, I see a lady standing next to me. She's tall. No, wait; I look down and she's wearing these bright-red shoes with heels as long as screwdrivers. She looks about my mom's age, but it's hard to tell because she's wearing loads of makeup. Her eyes are surrounded by smoky blackness, making the blue centers shine like beacons. Long, black waves of hair cascade over her shoulders and down her back. She must work here because Nick is setting a drink down without even asking her what she wants.

She mixes the amber liquid around the glass with her middle finger. Her painted nails are chipped and cracked, but the color that remains matches her shoes.

"Yeah, I'm okay, just tired." I look around and see Captain is still sitting with King. King is talking in small bursts while Captain looks bored. I think they are almost done, so we can go home.

"How old are you?" she asks, taking her whiskey fingers and pushing back the hair out of my face. I wonder if I'll smell like booze when I get home. "Yeah, you're just a kid, aren't you? What are you doing out so late? This ain't a regular stop for you, is it, honey?"

I shoot another glance over to Captain, and he takes his eyes off King for a second to look back. I think he sees me with this lady, but I don't know.

"Is that your dad?" she asks.

"No. No, I just work for him. Just here on business, that's all." I finally notice that my food has been sitting in front of me. I start to fidget with my silverware.

"Yeah, I'm just here on business too," she says, grabbing a fry and slowly angling it toward her mouth. *Does she work here? Are the fries cold?* I try focusing on my food, but I'm seriously nervous, and waves of tension roll through me.

"Roxy!" King barks out. "Take care of the kid, will ya? Give him whatever he wants."

I lean back and point to my plate to show him that I already have food.

"I don't think that's what he means." Roxy laughs. "Don't worry about it. His name may be King, but mainly he's just a joker." She pats me on the back and adds, "Enjoy your burger, sweetie. And get some sleep when you get home."

I'm relieved as she walks away, and I dig into my burger. Captain clamps his hand down on my shoulder and says, "Meet me out at the boat in five minutes." He and

King slip behind the faded purple curtain next to the stage. I feel for the knife in my pocket.

What a night.

We make the trip back to Warren in silence. I don't know what to call him. *Captain? George?* I steal glances at him as he steers the boat. I can see it now, the strong cheekbones, the chiseled nose and piercing eyes. I don't know why I've never noticed before. *Captain is Gene's brother. Gene's brother is a pirate, and he knows my dad.*

15

PLAYING CHICKEN

Saturday night, August 21

"Where have you been going at night?" My mom is standing in my bedroom doorway in her white dress, arms crossed tightly, a dishtowel hanging from her shoulder.

"What?" I sit up, my mind racing for excuses. I glance at the clock—5:43 p.m.

"Every night you've been coming home late, and you sleep all day; what's going on, Jake? I deserve to know."

"Nothing. Nothing's going on . . . I've been hanging out with Tommy. We've been night fishing, honest." The lie spills from my lips easily and seems to work as my mom uncrosses her arms and turns to leave. *It's almost the truth.*

"I'm going to visit Gene tonight. You should come with me. You haven't seen him in days." She says this over her shoulder, and a stab of guilt burns in my stomach. *I want to see him, but I can't look him in the eye. Not while I'm pirating with his brother. He'll know.*

"I can't go."

"And why not?" She swings around, eyes burning.

"I just can't. I can't see him like that. I hate hospitals. I'll see him when he gets out. Honest. He's getting out soon, right?"

"Well, he was, Jake. But he got this infection, so they are keeping him until it clears up. I know he'd love to see you."

"No!" I turn and stare out my window until she leaves, and I can hear her sounds of exasperation. I imagine her eyes rolling with disgust as she heads downstairs.

I feel torn into all these little pieces right now. I'm carrying them around, trying to figure out how they'll fit back together. I remember what Gene said about just dealing with what's in front of you at the time. *Just save the diner. That's what's in front of me right now.*

I lock the door to my room, pull out the cigar box, and open it. Captain finally paid me last night. I pull the wad of twenties from my jeans and toss it on the bed, emptying the rest of the money from the cigar box on top of that. Methodically I arrange the bills in four piles; twenties, tens, fives, and ones.

$2,368.

It's more money than I've ever had in my life, and still it's not even a quarter of what I need to earn in the next ten days. I do the math in my head and realize that even if I keep working with Captain, I will only make another three thousand by the end of the month. That's about half of what we owe. I wonder if it will be enough.

Keep at it, Jakeman; good things will come. My father's words echo in my head.

Four and a half hours later, I'm sitting on the seawall down by Kenyon's Dock, waiting for Captain to pick me up. It's quiet, except for a few clangs of the buoys echoing across the water.

Suddenly, I feel a giant hand pressing down on my shoulder.

"What the hell!" I try to get up, but whoever it is has me pinned down, and I can't even turn my head to see who it is.

"Don't worry," the voice says. "I just want to talk, that's all."

He slowly releases his death grip on my shoulder but leaves his hand there, warning me not to run. After a few seconds he lets go and sits down next to me on the seawall with a groan. Delvecchio laughs in a sick and twisted way as he settles in. I'm shaking like a leaf.

"What do you want?" My voice cracks.

"Just curious, that's all. I'm wondering what a kid your age is doing sitting out by the water this late at night."

"Me? I . . . uh . . . I just come out here listening for the fish, that's all. See if they're jumping. Maybe I'll go get my fishing rod."

"Fishing, huh?" Delvecchio looks out over the water, working the toothpick around his mouth. "What if I was to say that I thought you were out here waiting for somebody?"

How does he know?

"Me?" I say, searching for words.

Delvecchio tosses his toothpick toward the water. "Yes. I think you're waiting for somebody to come pick you up, and you and that person are gonna go out, under the cover of darkness, and you're gonna dig quahogs. Polluted quahogs. That's what I think."

"I'm not waiting for anybody . . . I swear." I'm freaking out because any second now Captain is going to pull up in his big gray boat, and I'll be sitting here on the seawall with Delvecchio. I pull my digital watch out and press the button a few times, sending a blue-green warning into the blackness. I hope he sees it. "It's late," I say. "I gotta go home."

"Look, Jake, I know you're not a pirate. Hell, you're

not even in high school. I'm after the guy you work for. He's a bad man, Jake, and I need your help to bring him down." Delvecchio looks at his own watch. 10:35.

"How do you know my name?"

"It's a small town, Jake. I know everybody. Now, tell me where George is working. Where are you selling the stuff?"

I feel like saying, *Same place as you, you bald-headed jerk.* But I know that he'll probably shoot me and dump my body in the river. "I really just came down here to listen for the fish, I swear. I don't know any George."

Delvecchio pulls a card out of his shirt pocket, writes a number down on the back, and hands it to me. "You give that number a call when you're ready to talk." I take the card, but he doesn't let go, and our eyes meet. "Just remember, Jake, this here is a courtesy visit. If I catch you doing bad things out there on the water, I might not remember that you're just a kid." He pats his gun in the holster at his belt.

He lets go of the card, and I jump up from where I'm sitting and take off down the street. When I am far enough away, I look back and Delvecchio is still sitting there, looking out over the water, waiting.

The first night, Captain told me about the alternate pickup spot. It was for emergencies only, and I figure this is about as good an emergency as any. I hop the fence and jog through the sewer plant toward the end of the pier.

Before I can even catch my breath, I can see Captain's boat pulling up. I jump aboard and we slip quietly out of the river.

As we make the turn past Rumstick Rock, I'm waiting for Captain to duck under the black shroud, but instead he kills the engines and turns to face me. "I thought I told you never to bring that watch?"

"I . . . er . . ."

"Relax, kid. You did the right thing. I got the warning. You're turning into a real pirate." Captain gives me a crooked smile. "So what does he know?"

So I tell him what Delvecchio knows, and he fidgets from side to side, his left eye twitching while his shoulder lifts, rotates, and releases in a quirky way, like his eyes and shoulders are all connected somehow.

Twenty minutes later, I am listening to the engines strain as the dredge tears its way across the polluted floor of the Providence River. It's the first haul of the night, so I have about five or ten minutes to chill out and wait. Captain doesn't like me milling about on deck, so I usually hang out down belowdecks in the bow cabin. The cabin is small, with two porthole windows painted black, a polished wooden floor, and a couple of padded triangular benches that seem like beds for toddlers. I crouch down, using a couple life jackets to rest my back against the wall where the beds come together, and shut the door tight.

No air. No light. I feel like an astronaut in a space capsule, hurtling through the dark. I feel for the tiny switch above my head and instantly my capsule is filled with warm yellow light.

I push at the large swollen blister between my right thumb and forefinger. I got it from hauling rope because my skin is still soft, but right now it's tight with liquid. I have to drain it.

I reach into my pocket to get my knife, and my fingers wrap around a triangular wad of paper the size of a couple of quarters. I pull it out and hold it to the light. It's from Darcy. I know it. Only Darcy would spend the time making all these intricate folds like an origami ninja. She must have slipped it into my pocket this morning. It takes me a while to open without ripping it.

Dear Jake,
Tommy told me what you've been doing and I think it's really stupid. Stupid and brave. (Don't blame him for telling me—I coaxed it out of him. You should know he folds easily under pressure.) I don't know whether to hug you or smash you upside the head with

a frying pan. I know we have to save the diner, but working for a crook, really?

Anyway, I've got some ideas of my own. Don't get mad, but it involves your mom (all of us, actually). She has already agreed, sort of. I'll tell you all about it tomorrow. You're gonna love it.

Be careful,
Darcy

I can feel my heartbeat in my ears. The floor beneath me drops away, and I'm floating in zero gravity. I close my eyes and let the feeling overtake me.

Buzzzzzzzzzzzzzzz. Buzz. Buzzzzzzzzzz!

The alarm!

I crash back to earth, scramble from my seat, and bang my head on the door as I rush out of the cabin. The alarm is going off, and that means that the clam cops are on us. *What do I do? Cut the ropes! Grab one of the machetes and cut the ropes to the dredge.*

Captain is working the controls and swearing like a madman. Our boat is bogging down with the strain of the dredge, and I can see the blue swirling lights of the DEM boat coming right at us full speed. I reach for the machete strapped to the side of the console. The clam cops are a hundred yards away and coming fast. I whip around toward the taut lines of the dredge post and swing the steel blade with everything I've got. The rope pops horrifically. The boat jumps forward, sending me hard into the rear well. The oncoming cops' boat slides into the space we just left.

They almost rammed us.

The clam cop is yelling through the loudspeaker, but I can't make out what he is saying. Something about *disengage* and *boarding*. Our boat is making a wide arc. I'm waiting for Captain to take the wheel.

Oh, crap.

He's not moving. I see him, sprawled on the deck with a huge lump on his head. He must have hit the dredge post when the boat lurched.

I want to help him, but I can't right now. I throttle the engines down. The clam cops are pulling aside, and they're about to board.

"Where is he?" It's Delvecchio. His eyes are wide as silver dollars as he looks right at me. His partner is reaching for our bow cleat with a rope in his hand. Delvecchio finally sees Captain, unconscious on the deck. A smile cuts across Delvecchio's face as he grabs at the gun strapped to his hip, blue lights flickering everywhere. *He's going to kill us.*

I grab the wheel and shove all my weight into the throttle. The boat shoots forward like a missile. I point us toward the middle of the bay, toward safety, out of the river and away from Delvecchio. I turn on the deck lights for a second and see that Captain is crumpled at the stern, the purple knot on his head protruding.

"Oh, crap," I say under my breath as I realize we just did a hundred-and-eighty degree turn, and we are heading right at the clam cops. My dad always said, "The best defense is a good offense." So I go on offense. I keep the boat going straight at them like a fighter pilot. I can still hear the alarm buzzing in the bow cabin, just faintly, above the scream of the engines. Delvecchio is still bearing down on us. It's like the game of chicken Tommy and I used to play on our bikes, except now it's boats and they're big and fast, and someone is going to get killed.

I should turn. Wait. I gotta turn. Wait.

He turns first, to the east. I crank the wheel and we spin, sending the stern of the boat out wide. Captain slides across the deck. Delvecchio is still yelling into his loudspeaker, and his partner is pulling a rifle out of the gun rack. My heart is pounding and my hands are shaking. I'm wondering if I'll go to jail or even worse, get shot.

My boat is faster. I peg the throttle again and the boat explodes out of the water. I can't look back. I'm just holding on. *Get your bearings. Where's Prudence Island?*

There, I see it.

I'm flying toward the narrow channel between Prudence and Patience Islands. The tachometer reads

9,000 rpm. We must be doing eighty miles an hour. I look back and the clam cops are still chasing us. Their blue flashing light is getting smaller. I drape the black shroud over the instrument panel and go into stealth mode, steering on a heading toward Newport Harbor, where we can get lost in the forest of sailboats.

As we slide under the Newport Bridge, I can no longer see the blue lights.

"I've lost them. I did it!" I am screaming now and I look back at Captain. He's still passed out. He may be dead. *Try to stay calm. Think.*

I pull back on the throttle as we come into the harbor, and the boat slows to a crawl. I yank the fishing poles out of the cabin and set them into the holders as I weave my way through the maze of sailboats. I can see Bowen's Wharf, where all the bars and restaurants are, so I slip in between a mess of lines and tie off. The boat looks clean, except for Captain lying there in a heap.

I've got to get help. I've got to get this boat out of here.

"How's it goin' there? You catch anything?" A man wanders down the dock toward me.

"I need help. Help me get him out of the boat," I say to him.

"Thassa nice boat." The guy looks over the side and takes a step back, almost falling into the water. "Except for that. What the hell happened to him?" That's when I notice the large bottle dangling in the guy's hand. He's definitely drunk.

"Help me get him onto the dock!" I yell, pulling on Captain's arms, hoisting him to the side. The guy throws his bottle in the water and climbs aboard.

"Less just shove 'im over onto the dock and drag 'im up the ramp," the guy says. "What were you fishing for?"

"Stripers. Come on, lift and watch his head." The drunk guy is not paying attention, and Captain's head bangs against the pylon with a dull thud as we come out of the boat.

"You using bait or lures, poppers or what?" Captain's boots drag over the wooden boards as we make our way up the gangway.

At the dockmaster's shack, I see a pay phone and reach in my pocket. I don't have any change, so I frantically reach into Captain's pocket. It's creepy. He's like a dead man except he's still breathing. I find a coin.

"Nine-one-one. What is the nature of your call, police, fire, or ambulance?"

"Ambulance!" I scream.

"Calm down, sir. Where are you?"

"I'm at Bowen's Wharf, at the dockside where the fishing boats are tied up."

The drunk guy leans into my ear now. "Nine-one-one's a free call, ya know."

"Give me an address, sir. Are you at a residence, a street name, house number?"

"I'm not on a street, I'm at Bowen's, and Captain's been passed out for twenty minutes."

"Help is on the way. Stay on the line. I want to ask you a few questions. Is he still breathing?"

I don't want to answer anything, so I hang up the phone, turn around, and the drunk guy is leaning into me like he's going to fall asleep on my shoulder.

"You call the cops? Ahh, I gotta get out of here," he slurs, grabbing the unused quarter out of the change slot.

"No, I called an ambulance. Thanks for your help."

He stumbles away, almost falling off the wharf.

It's a long ten minutes before the ambulance arrives. I'm propping up Captain with my shoulder, trying to wake him. Two people in white shirts, carrying large orange medical boxes jump out of the ambulance. The spotlights from the vehicle throw long shadows across the wharf.

"What took you so long?" I say to the short redheaded guy who is grabbing Captain's wrist and checking his watch. He ignores my question.

The other paramedic, a thin Hispanic woman, is lifting Captain's eyelids and flashing a small light into his eyes. "How long has he been out?"

"Twenty minutes, maybe more," I answer, guessing. The paramedics lift Captain onto the stretcher. "Where are you taking him?"

"You all through? I gotta take a report here." A voice from behind startles me, and I bang into the stretcher and fall down, almost landing on Captain. A hand reaches under my armpit and pulls me to my feet.

A cop. Two cops, in fact.

"Easy, kid. I think they only have one stretcher." He's still holding my arm, and his grip is tight.

"I—I thought I just called for an ambulance," I stammer, looking over at the paramedics, who have Captain on the stretcher and are moving toward the ambulance.

Oh, crap, what do I tell them?

"It's just routine." The cop waves a pad and steps back into view. "You want to tell me what happened here?" The other cop is circling the wharf, checking out some of the boats.

"We were walking up the ramp, and Captain fell and bumped his head on the gangway railing."

"Where, right here on this dock? Is that your father?" The cop is making notes on his pad when out of the corner of my eye I see the drunk guy coming back up the wharf, and he's staggering worse than before.

"That kidza hellofa fisherman!" He starts yelling at the cops. "Bestest I ever seen." He's got a new bottle, and he's waving it in the air, coming straight at us. He's off his rocker, and both cops step toward him, hands resting on their holsters.

"Whoa, sir! Put the bottle down and step back."

"Whaddya mean? Thas my friend you're arresin." The bottle falls out of his hand and explodes on the ground. The cops move in quickly, and I take the opportunity to slip away into the shadows of the fishing vessels.

My heart is pounding out of my chest as I dodge behind some parked cars. The cops are still dealing with the drunk as he wrestles and squirms on the ground.

I hope he doesn't mention the boat.

I sneak back to the boat. Once I'm aboard, I push off silently and drift into the harbor.

When I'm far enough away, I start the engines and head for home.

I'm not going to make it to fifteen at this rate.

16

STRIPERS

Sunday evening, August 22

It's five thirty in the evening, and I'm at Deluca's Pharmacy, picking up my mom's pills. They're called Valium, and she says they calm her nerves, but I think they just make her space out, and if anyone needed their nerves calmed down, it would be me. I mean, every time I turn around somebody gets hurt, and right now I'm still shaky after ditching those cops last night.

"How's your mother feeling, Jake?" Mr. Deluca asks while squirting the cherry syrup and Coca-Cola mixture into a fountain glass.

"She's good," I lie with a smile. I wanted to say that she seems like she's on another planet and that she wants to give up the diner and move to the middle of the freakin' desert and get a job at a grocery store, but I don't think that's what he wants to hear.

"I worry about her working so hard." He pulls the stem on the soda fountain and fills the glass with bubbly water. I watch as he stirs the concoction with a long silver spoon. He hands me the cherry Coke with one hand and uses the other to push back the quarters I set on the wooden counter. "This one's on me."

"Thanks, Mr. Deluca." I lift the Coke from the counter and squeeze into one of the small booths by the window, waiting for Mr. Deluca's son, Ziggy, to fill my mom's prescription.

I drink the Coke and watch the cars through the window as they make their way down Main Street. I let the soda swish around my mouth before swallowing. I'm hoping Mr. Deluca ignores me because I really don't feel like talking right now.

I hear the back door buzz and turn around to see Ziggy walking toward me with a small paper bag and a smile on his face.

"Here you go, Jake. This ought to last her through the end of next month."

"Thanks." I get up from the booth to pay for the prescription, but he's standing in the way, like he wants to talk. Ziggy is a short guy, and it feels weird looking down at him like he's a little kid.

"Boy, I could use someone like you working here." He turns to his dad. "If Jake worked here, we wouldn't need the ladder at all." Mr. Deluca is smiling at us as Ziggy straightens up next to me and reaches his arm up as high as he can. "You got good genes, Jake, not like some of us." He pretends to whisper in my ear, thumbing at his dad.

He hands me the bag and manipulates the antique cash register, and the mechanical numbers flip around until they're all zeros.

"I have to pay you. Mom sent me with money to pay," I say this, pleading.

"No money from you, Jake, not now, not ever. Your dad, God bless him, was one of my closest friends."

"Thanks, Mr. Deluca."

"I hear you've been fishing with Gene Hassard. How's that going?"

"Everything's cool," I lie again.

"Drop a half a bag of chowders off sometime, will you, Jake? My wife wants to make some chowder."

"Sure, Mr. Deluca," I call back, bells ringing as the door shuts behind me.

I step out onto the sidewalk and bump hard into a shoulder. *Smack.* It's Captain. He's dancing on one leg to keep his beer from spilling on the sidewalk. There's still a huge bump on his forehead. He looks like hell, like he's been drunk since the accident.

"Come with me," he says, leading me toward his truck

parked nearby. I want to run in the other direction. I want to be anywhere else right now.

"I, uh, gotta get these pills to my mom," I say, holding up the bag. Captain is looking at Mr. Deluca, who is now outside, removing the flag from the front of the building and watching us. The six o'clock fire horn goes off behind the town hall. *A sign. Is that another warning from my dad?*

"Come on, we'll swing by the diner," Captain says.

Mr. Deluca continues watching as I climb into the truck. I smile and wave, but he still looks concerned as he folds his flag into a precise triangle. The truck hammers out into traffic, forcing a line of cars to slow down. Captain takes a tug on his beer and stares hard at the bag in my hand.

"What kind of pills?"

"Valium, for her nerves." I'm wondering if Captain is going to take my mom's pills.

"What happened? How'd I get this egg on my head?" The locks click shut on the doors of the truck, and I'm thinking Captain is going to kill me and dump me in the river.

"I had to cut us loose before Delvecchio T-boned us, and when I did, the boat lurched forward, and you must have slammed into the dredge post. He was going to shoot you, you know." Captain closes his eyes for a long second, and the truck drifts across the yellow line. A car horn blares, and he opens his eyes, startled.

"I don't remember much."

I'm sweating and I can feel it beading on my forehead. My left ear is hot. When I'm nerved up, my ears get hot and red and I think they're going to melt right off.

"What did you tell the cops about me when they talked to you at the hospital?"

"I never went to the hospital. . . . I told the cops at the dock that we were fishing and you actually fell on the gangway."

"That was almost my story," he says in a slur. "Good thinking bringing me into Newport Harbor. I was out cold and you saved the boat. All that works for me." He turns onto Water Street. "I want to take you out fishing tonight."

"I can't go dredging tonight." The word *dredging* spills out of my mouth like rancid milk, and I can see Captain is offended.

"Not dredging, Jake, fishing . . . fishing for fish. The stripers are running, and I thought we could catch a couple. You know, for fun. Maybe the diner could have a striped bass special."

Two new fishing poles are neatly set in pole holders in the bed of the truck; his tackle box is set up and he's ready to fish.

"All right," I say. It doesn't seem like I have a choice.

Twenty minutes later we are heading out, and the back of the boat is filled with buckets of bait and chum. I'm assuming he brought me along to throw chum and cut bait while he catches stripers. All the while I feel like a hostage. We slow down near the large red channel marker floating in front of Ginalski's Marina. I'm wicked paranoid.

"You think Delvecchio is out looking for us, Cap?"

"That prick is always looking for me. Don't worry about it, though. You're just a kid."

"Yeah, but I don't look like a kid, especially in the dark. They had guns, you know."

"I know," he says.

"We can always outrun them, I guess."

Captain turns to me and unbuttons the top two buttons of his shirt, revealing an ugly hole just below his collarbone. It's filled with skin that looks like wood putty. "You can't outrun bullets." He laughs.

"You got shot?" I get dizzy and my stomach goes sour, thinking I could have been shot the other night. I could have been killed.

"Tie us up there." Captain buttons his shirt and points to the red channel marker. He empties a five-gallon bucket of chopped fish overboard, then dips the white bucket into the water and rinses it out before handing it to me. He points to the electronic fish finder on the console, where a series of red dots move slowly on the screen.

"We're on 'em, Jake. This trench is full of fish." He acts like our conversation didn't even take place, and I'm still standing there in shock, holding the bait bucket. "Come on, snap out of it. It's a great night, and we're gonna have a blast. Forget about last night. Besides that little runt that works for Delvecchio said he's at the racetrack tonight, playing the horses. He'll tell me anything I want to know for a hundred bucks," he says with a smile.

He sets up my fishing rod for me, just like my dad used to. He attaches the bait to my hook, and the sinker slides to the bottom. I can tell he's suffering because he's stumbling around the boat, but he insists on doing everything. Maybe he's being nice because I saved his boat. Either way, it helps me relax, and suddenly I can't wait to get my line in the water. I haven't caught a striped bass since I went fishing with my dad two summers ago.

It's starting to get dark as the sun dips below the horizon, and Captain throws on his deck lights. The area around the boat comes to life with fluorescent baitfish scattering across the surface. Occasionally I hear the sound of the water getting stirred up as if someone ran an oar through it.

"Hear that, Jake?" Captain says in an excited tone. "That's the sound of striped bass. That's the sound of money. Striped bass with dollar bills attached, swirling around the boat. This place is hot with fish."

I drop my bait from the stern as the tide reaches for my line, pulling it down with the weight of the lead sinker. I can feel it hit bottom with a bump. My hand is on the drag of the reel, and I am releasing it slowly, when suddenly a fish slams the bait and runs fifty yards. It's all I can do to loosen the drag as the powerful fish nearly pulls me out of the boat.

"Hit him with the hook! Hit him with the hook!" Captain screams. I dip the pole tip and yank hard to set the hook into the fish's mouth and finally feel the true weight of the fish at the end of my line. *I've angered it now.*

"Don't lose it. That's a big fish, could be thirty pounds or more. *Don't you lose it, Jake!* Keep your tip up. That's a seventy-five dollar fish you've got there."

I'm holding on with everything I've got, and I think this fish is going to drag the boat, but I remember we're tied to the red can. Knowing that I've got a seventy-five-dollar fish at the end of my line is not making it any easier. I think Captain might throw me overboard if I lose it. I'm holding on for dear life as this fish is swimming for freedom.

Captain is at the rail with a stainless-steel gaff. I can see the sharp hook at the end glinting in the deck lights. After only a five- or ten-minute struggle that seems like an eternity, the fish finds the surface and starts rolling over with fatigue. It's the biggest fish I've ever caught. I can see the last bit of life lifting from its body with shivering shakes.

We are both tired now, and I am leaning against the rail, staring at this beautiful fish, stripes like a tiger down its sides, long, dark-green tail slowly turning in the tide, when suddenly the gaff disturbs the moment in a flash. *Smack.* The steely point catches its underbelly, and the fish is brought back to life, using all of its force to reject death as Captain hauls it into the boat and drops it to the deck. It makes a loud thud, thrashes for a second or two, and then rests. Only its gills make an effort to express life, opening and closing, gasping for liquid air. *I know how he feels.*

"That's a beauty, Jake." Captain's admiring the fish as his reel starts singing. *Zzzz.* He drops the gaff next to the fish.

"Get a bait in the water, Jake. It's gonna be a fun night."

I unhook the giant, admiring its silver and black stripes. I wish I could send it back, but it's too late now.

"Get the gaff ready, Jake. Get your line in the water, Jake. Get that fish in the hold."

I'm used to taking orders, even multiple orders, but this seems ridiculous. In two hours we have seventeen stripers, all more than thirty pounds, sitting on top of ice in the storage compartment below deck.

"I bet we got about five hundred pounds of striped bass here, Jake. I'll call Hank at Narragansett Fish Factory. Maybe we can get a good price."

I realize this was never just about going out and having a good time fishing. Captain had said fishing "for fun." *Yeah, right.* But I guess I might as well get paid to fish, even if it is just like pirating.

Captain punches it, and we are in Providence in eight minutes, idling up to the dock. The Fish Factory restaurant is right on the water, and there's a ton of people sitting at tables outside, eating, drinking, and laughing.

Captain leaves me there in the boat and shuffles up to the red building. I lift the hatch and begin removing the fish one by one. The slippery scales force me to squat and reach deep into their huge gills to lift them out of the hold. The people in the restaurant look on, some in amazement at all the fish we caught. Others seem disgusted by our appearance, as we're covered in fish scales and striper blood.

Captain is walking back down the gangway, followed by three men. One of them is wearing a green sweater and pale-yellow shorts. I assume it's Hank because the other two are carrying large green fish totes, dressed in aprons and white kitchen clothes.

"Who's the kid?"

"Jake, meet Hank," Captain says, thumbing toward the guy who has already got one of his white sneakers resting on the side of our boat. "That's Jake. He's a great fisherman. John Cole's kid."

"Jesus Christ, John Cole's kid? No wonder you're a good fisherman; your dad could catch anything in that bay. I heard what happened to him. It's a damned shame."

"Yes, sir," I say, pulling the last of the fish out of the hold. People from the restaurant are leaning over the railing now, looking on, some of them snapping pictures of all the fish. I'm beaming with pride, but Captain looks irritated.

"I'll take it all, George," Hank says with a fake reluctant tone to his voice.

"Nothing's fresher than that fish; Christ, that's sushi-grade, Hank."

"I'll be able to sell it for sure. How about a buck a pound?" Hank smiles.

Captain jumps on board and starts the engines.

"Jake, get the lines."

"What do you mean, Cap?"

"Get the lines!"

I release the bowline and start for the stern. Hank is now holding the rope.

"Wait, George, how about two bucks a pound?"

"Jake, tie up the bowline."

We move the fish up the ramp to the fish house, past the people out on the deck. Hank weighs the fish on a stainless-steel scale.

"Five hundred and forty-seven pounds."

He starts hammering on his pocket calculator. Hank reaches into his pocket and pulls out the biggest roll of hundred-dollar bills I've ever seen, and we get paid in cash, right there on the spot. Captain holds the money out in front of me.

"Check it out," he says. "And we were just fishing . . . kids' stuff."

"Can I use your bathroom?" I ask Hank.

"Straight through the double doors to the kitchen, then turn right. Use the employee restroom. It's much cleaner." He laughs as I head up the gangway.

I head into one of the stalls and lock the door. *Wow, we*

made over a thousand bucks, just from fishing for one night.
I pee and zip up.

As I walk back through the kitchen, everything is in chaos. All the workers are yelling in Spanish, half of them running out the back door, others running toward the front. The door swings open, and red and blue police lights flicker against the stainless-steel tables and shelving. I start to panic and follow the cooks out the door, ducking into the shadow of the Dumpsters.

"Qué pasa?" One of the cooks nudges me.

"I don't speak Spanish," I say as I squat down next to him.

"Who they looking for?" he says.

There are cops everywhere, but not police. The green blazers and pickup trucks tell me it's the DEM. They have this guy laid out on the hood of the truck, and they are slapping handcuffs on him. His face is pushed down, and I can't see it, but I already know who it is. Delvecchio is leaning over Captain, talking in his ear as he wrenches his arms back. I can hear Captain groaning.

Delvecchio looks over and spots me. Our eyes lock for an instant, and he gives me the slightest nod, as if telling me to get the hell out of here.

I run.

17
LOST AND FOUND
Sunday night, August 22

I come to a stop on Gano Street and rest on a bench. The single streetlamp throws a blanket of light around me. I'm breathing hard. *What do I do now? This is so messed up. Help me, Dad.*

"Aha! Visitors!" The voice is filled with joy. A homeless woman is wheeling a shopping cart out of the shadows. The cart overflows with bottles, cans, an old backpack, and some dirty stuffed animals. I'm thinking of running again, but she seems harmless enough, and I don't have any more run left in me. She parks the cart and falls heavily onto the bench. "Welcome."

"Welcome?" I ask, sliding away from her, but too tired to get up.

"Yeah, welcome to my home." She slides a dirty thumb proudly over some letters carved into the bench.

"This is your *house*?" I stand and take a step back.

"Please, please, sit down. I don't bite. I never have guests." She smiles warmly and I sit.

"So are you Mary Carol?" I glance at the letters she's thumbing.

"I'm just Mary. Carol's gone." She pats the name tenderly.

"So, really, this is like . . . your home?"

"Only for the last seven years. Before this I had a great bench over on Wickenden Street, but it got too fancy for me." She opens a tinfoil wrapper with half a sandwich inside and brings it to her nose. "Tuna . . . *blech*! It never lasts in this heat." She tosses the sandwich into the garbage drum and folds the foil into a small neat square. "So where are *you* living?"

"Me? I live over in Warren."

"Warren. Great town. You gotta house?" She takes a sip of water from a scratched-up soda bottle, then offers it to me.

"No, thanks." I wave my hand. "Yeah we've got a house, well, sort of. It's a small apartment above a diner. It's not that big."

"Probably a whole lot bigger than this bench." She laughs. "Above a diner . . . how great is that? I can just imagine waking up to those smells every morning . . . bacon, eggs, home fries . . . whooo-wee." She looks off dreamily.

"Well, we used to have a real house, with a yard and a garden and stuff, but the bank . . . you know . . . they take stuff."

"The bank can't get nothing from me." She winks. "So who's *we*? You got family or something?"

"Sort of. I mean, I live with my mom." I don't want to start explaining how my dad disappeared, so I keep that to myself.

"Well, then, there you go! You got a family all right . . . a mom . . . doesn't get any better than that. I should know . . . I'm a mom myself."

"You're a mom? Where are your kids?"

"It was just Carol. Only Carol." She runs her hand tenderly across the name carved into the bench. With the other hand she reaches down into her pocket and pulls out a quarter and hands it to me. "You see that pay phone over there?"

"Yeah."

"Call your mother."

"I can't take your money."

"Call . . . your . . . mother," she says, leaning closer.

I take the quarter and walk across the street to the pay phone.

On the third ring she answers. "Mom?"

"Jake, where are you? What's happened?" She's panicked.

"I'm in Providence. I . . . I need you."

"Are you okay? I'll come and get you."

I tell her where I am and hang up the phone. When I look back at the bench, Mary is gone. I didn't even get a chance to thank her.

Twenty minutes later we're driving home. My mom has one hand on the wheel, and she's raking her fingers through her hair, and her lip is quivering. She doesn't say anything.

"Don't you want to know why I was in Providence in the middle of the night?" I can barely get the words out. I'm choked up.

She takes a deep, long breath through her nose. "Of course I want to know. What mother wouldn't want to know where her fourteen-year-old son is in the middle of the night?" She's talking at the windshield and gesturing wildly with her hand. "I have a son who thinks it's okay to be out all night, and that his mother wouldn't care?"

We come to a red light and I turn to face her. "I've been trying to raise the money, you know . . . the money we owe for the diner. I know you're ready to give it up and move to Arizona, and you cry every day. Dad would have never given up. I'm just doing what he'd do."

My mom swerves into an abandoned parking lot and

rests her head on the steering wheel. When she looks up at me, there are tears streaming down her face. *Here we go.*

"Jake, do you *really* think I want to give up the diner? I know I've been a mess, but that diner is the only thing that keeps me going. Being there every day is like being with your dad. It's a piece of him. I can't let that go. The Riptide is part of us." She can barely say the words. "I just don't know what else to do. What can we do? We owe too much money, and the bank won't loan us a dime, and we can't ask any more from our friends . . ."

"But Mom, I've been making money, lots of it. I've been out working nights with Gene's brother, but . . . he just got arrested."

"You think I didn't know you were up to something? I knew you were out on the bay every night. Muddy clothes don't *magically* get cleaned every day. Believe me, Jake; I couldn't sleep until I knew you were home. Kids your age are stealing, vandalizing, and getting into all kinds of trouble. I don't know how to handle *everything*. I even asked Darcy what was up. Of course she wouldn't say a word, and Tommy avoids me like the plague. I didn't know what to do." She takes my hands into hers and holds them tight. She's shaking them as she speaks. "I can't lose you too. You promise me you will *never* do that again. *You promise me.* Look at me, Jake. *Promise.*"

I lift my head and look at her and she's not crying anymore. She looks strong. She looks like she used to before my dad disappeared. I throw my arms around her and bury my head into her shoulder. She pulls me in tight, and I start convulsing with tears as if she's squeezing them out of me.

"Finally. Thank you, Jake."

This is it. The first time I've hugged her since dad went missing.

A dark, twisted knot, this mass in my stomach that I've felt for a long time, is working its way up to my throat. I cough and gag and I can feel it leaving. And now all I can feel is my mother's arms.

I'm not alone anymore.

18

CONFESSIONS

Sunday night, August 22

When we arrive back home, my mom heads into the kitchen of the diner and flicks the lights on. I follow her in.

"What are you making?" I ask, plopping down on one of the stools.

"Late breakfast." She looks at the clock on the wall and laughs. "Or maybe an early one. Hungry?"

"Starved."

"Did you know that your dad made breakfast for me when I came home from the hospital with you?" She points with the spatula to one of a hundred faded Polaroids pinned to the wall above her. "That's you and dad. You were three days old."

"That's us?" I lean forward in my seat. It's a picture of my dad sitting at this very counter, holding a tiny little baby wrapped up in a blue blanket. My mom pulls the photo down and hands it to me. My dad is surrounded by a bunch of his buddies, and they all have big cigars hanging from their mouths. To the right of my father, I see Gene, and directly behind him is another man. *George Hassard.* I drop the photo on the counter like it's a hot plate burning my fingers. I guess I shouldn't be surprised, but it's weird seeing Captain standing next to my dad, and it's even weirder seeing him standing next to me at three days old. "Did Dad know George?"

"Of course. He and Gene and your dad were best friends. They were inseparable. They grew up together. They went out quahogging together, camping together . . . everything," my mom says with a tight smile. "George was the best man at our wedding."

My head is spinning. I can't imagine my dad being friends with Captain, never mind his *best* friend. I'm staring at the photo now, looking at George Hassard. He looks so young, tanned and smiling. His shirt is unbuttoned and I can't see his scar.

"What happened? I only met this guy for the first time eleven days ago," I say.

"He turned up now and then over the years, but it always ended in arguments. Your father would never really tell me much." She pours pancakes on the griddle and puts the bowl down carefully. Turning back to me, she places both elbows on the counter. "George is not a bad man, Jake, but he does bad things." She places her hands on my forearms and opens her eyes wide. "Even so, you need to stay away from him. I know you were just doing what you thought you had to, but it's not worth it."

"How come I've never seen this before?" I ask, holding the Polaroid up to my mom's face.

"I just found it." My mom is watching me carefully as I study the photo. "I was packing up some things, and it was tucked between some pages in the photo album."

"Packing? You *are* giving up!" My voice gets loud.

"I said I *was* packing. I stopped. I couldn't do it." Her voice is cracking again as she waves her hands around the room. "This is all that your father left us."

"Yeah, this, and a bunch of debt."

"That's not fair, Jake." She looks at me and her eyes tighten. "You don't know the situation we were in. I signed on to that debt too, not just your father." She slides a plate of pancakes in front of me, but suddenly I'm not hungry anymore. "I was pregnant with you when he injured his back." She's looking at all the photos on the wall. "The only thing he enjoyed more than being a quahogger was cooking. So that's when he decided to build this diner."

"Yeah, I already know that."

"But what you don't know is this: Those jerks at the bank weren't about to give an injured fisherman money to build a diner. I mean, we already owed them a ton of money for the house."

"So he went to the Mafia?"

"No." She whips around to face me. "Well, yes . . . sort of. I mean they aren't really the Mafia like you see on television. We'd be wearing cement shoes by now, standing there at the bottom of the river." She lets out a nervous laugh.

"But they are going to take the diner, just like the bank took our house?"

"Business has been slow. I haven't been able to make the payments. I thought they would give us a break, with John gone and everything."

"Well *you* drive away all the customers," I say angrily, and get up from my stool and head over to one of the booths with my back to her.

"That's not fair!" I can hear her storming around the counter toward me. She slides into the booth and forces me to look at her. She's holding a clenched fist to her chest. "I lost my husband. Every time one of our customers walks in that door, I wait for your father to shout out a hello, or break into a story, but nothing comes, just silence." Her tears begin to flow again.

"Just wait here a second," I say, and run upstairs.

Seconds later I place the cigar box down on the table in front of her. She traces the lid with her finger.

"This was your father's. Where . . . where did you find this?"

"Open it."

She opens the lid carefully and her eyes go wide.

"Oh. Oh, my God. Jake, there must be thousands here," she says, lifting some of the bills.

"A little over two thousand. Not enough to keep them from taking the diner, though, is it?"

She throws her arms around me and nearly squeezes the breath out of me. It feels great. She pulls back and takes both my arms with her hands. "You know what you did is wrong, though, don't you?"

"Yeah, but not more wrong than them taking the diner," I say defensively.

"It doesn't matter what they do. It only matters what we do."

"So what are we going to do?"

"Well"—she claps her hands together—"Darcy had a pretty good idea, and I think we should do it."

The mention of Darcy shakes me. I wipe my face as if she might walk into the diner any second. "Yeah, what is it?"

My mom's eyes light up as she says, "A cabaret."

"What's a *cabaret*?"

"Well, we turn this diner into a fancy nightclub for a night. We have entertainment, dinner, drinks, candlelight . . . it'll be fun."

"*That's* Darcy's idea?"

"Oh, come on." She slaps my arm playfully. "It's a great idea. Robin will sing, and we'll charge twenty bucks a head, even fix the jukebox."

I haven't seen my mom this excited about anything in years, and I don't want to burst her bubble, but the math just doesn't add up. Even if we fill the place, at twenty bucks a head that'll be about fifteen hundred bucks. Not nearly enough to cover our debt.

"When?" I ask.

"Well, I was thinking. . . ." She starts pointing to the tabletop as if it's an invisible calendar. "The day after tomorrow is the big Barrington Beach opening, right?"

"Uh-huh."

"And all these quahoggers can't think of anything else right now. I swear that's all they talk about. So I was thinking the next night, Wednesday. We'll paint up a sign and leave it out on the street so everyone can see it."

The phone rings. *It's the police. They saw me.* I get flush with fever; my rib cage is about to burst. *Please don't let it be the cops.*

"Who could be calling at this hour?" My mom heads over to the phone, and I want to tell her not to pick it up, that it's a crank call, a salesman . . . anything. *Just don't pick up the phone!* I'm frozen in my seat.

My mom is real quiet on the phone, just listening, and I'm sure this is the end for me. *I'm going to jail.*

She hangs up the phone and carefully walks back over to the table, like she's afraid the floor might crack open and she'll fall through.

"It's Gene." Her eyes are red and tight with concern. "That was his sister, Ginny. He's gotten worse. The infection has spread through his bloodstream and . . ." Her hand goes up and covers her mouth. Her face contorts into a knot.

"I thought he was coming home."

"That's what we all thought, but they're not sure he's strong enough to fight it."

"What are you saying? That he could die? Who says he's not strong enough?" The room is spinning.

"The doctors . . . nobody. Nobody says he's not strong enough. Gene will be fine. Gene will be fine." My mom keeps repeating this over and over, like she's in some sort of trance.

I run up to my room, slam the door, and fall onto my bed, covering my face with my hands. I picture Gene on his boat, pulling the rake, looking strong and healthy. I hold that image in my mind for as long as I can.

Sleep overtakes me.

19
SHATTERED
Monday, August 23

I sleep all day.

20

INTO THE LION'S DEN

Tuesday morning, August 24

It's 4 a.m. . . . . It's 4 a.m. . . . . I bolt out of bed in a panic, the alarm still echoing in my head. My feet settle on the cold floor as I get my bearings. *Why am I up at four?*

Now I remember. Today is the Barrington Beach opening, and I'm gonna make it there after all.

I get dressed and take the stairs down into the kitchen. Through the window I can see my mom, Trax, and Robin going through the motions. The regulars are already in their seats, gulping down coffee and fueling up for the big day.

I rush around and, still fixing my shirt, grab two gallons of water, two loaves of bread from the pantry, and two large cans of beef stew. I remember to grab a can opener and throw it all in a large canvas bag.

"Where you going with all that?" Robin stares at the bag in my hand as she bangs through the double doors.

"Me? This? It's my lunch. It's going to be a long day," I say, hefting the bag.

"Are you working for Dave Becker today?"

"Yeah, sort of a last-minute thing," I lie.

"Is he coming in? I haven't seen him in years." She checks her hair in the reflection of the fridge.

"Ah, no. He doesn't eat breakfast. I'm meeting him at the dock." I leave the bag at the back door and head toward the dining room.

I squeeze past Trax and swipe a couple Danish and three bananas from behind the glass case next to the register.

"Some morning, huh, Skipper?" Trax lifts his glasses and wipes the sweat from his brow with his rolled-up shirtsleeve.

"It's the big day. Where's Darcy?'

"She's just a kid, Jake. Your mom's not going to have her come in at this hour."

"Just a kid?" I grunt. "I'm just a kid, and I'm here, aren't I?"

"Yeah, but you live here. That doesn't count." Trax studies the grill and counts the orders with his finger. "You want any breakfast?"

"No, thanks, Trax. I gotta run."

I duck out from behind the counter, shove a Danish in my mouth, and use my back to push through the double doors. As I bend down to pick up my bag, a pair of black Converse sneakers step into view.

"You're going to do it, aren't you?" She has her arms crossed just like my mom does when she's angry with me.

"Do what?" I try to go around her, but she keeps side-stepping and blocking my way.

"You're going to work the beach today." Darcy is stabbing her finger into my chest as she stands on the tips of her toes, trying to make eye contact as I look away. "You're taking Gene's boat, and you're going out there by yourself."

My eyes dart toward the double doors.

"Aha!" She says, bouncing on her toes. "I knew it." She grabs my shirt by the collar and pulls me down toward her. "Well, I got news for you, Stretch; I'm going with you."

"What?" For a millisecond the idea sounds pretty cool. Me and Darcy out on the boat together . . . but then I think of Gene and George and how they got hurt and how I couldn't forgive myself if anything happened to her too. "You can't come with me, Darce."

"I may not know much about quahogging, but if I can handle working in this place, I can handle counting a few quahogs."

I take Darcy by the arm and lead her out the back door so we can talk without being overheard. We stop short by the streetlight near the seawall.

"I have to do this alone. That's the way it's supposed to be."

"That is so lame. You know we're all in this together."

"Look, Darcy, I don't want you to get hurt."

"Even lamer." She's rolling her eyes at me.

"All right, here's the deal. When I'm out there, I have to be totally focused, and with you on board, who knows what I'll be thinking about? Plus, there aren't any girls out there."

"Oh, my God! Did you just say that?" Darcy is walking in circles, talking to herself. "He did. He just said there are no girls out there. No *girls!*"

"Darce?"

She circles back around and comes at me like a tiger, eyes flashing. "Now, you listen to me, I'm not just any girl. I'm the girl that's going to help you save this diner. You don't know what life was like for me before this place. You don't know . . ." Big pools of water are welling up in her eyes, and she keeps poking her finger into my chest.

"I do know." I slowly reach out and rub her arm. I can feel the rippled scars through her sweater. Darcy shudders slightly and looks at me, her eyes red and wet.

"Close your eyes," Darcy says, her voice quiet and small.

"What?"

"Just close your eyes."

I do as I'm told. I hear the sweater's zipper and the rustling of clothes. I nervously start talking, eyes still shut. "My mom told me your idea about the cabaret. I think it's great."

"You do?"

"Yeah, my mom is so excited about it. I haven't seen her this excited about anything in a while. She's been in a slump forever, and your idea totally pulled her out of it."

"Good. Okay, now . . . open your eyes."

"Whoa."

That's all I can say. Darcy shivers in the cold morning air, eyes wide, watching my face. She's wearing a tank top. Her pale skin glows softly in the light of the streetlamp. My eyes sweep down her arm, tracing each contour. The scars pull and stretch across her skin, reminding me of a partially deflated balloon. It's different and scary and like nothing I've ever seen, but it isn't ugly.

Suddenly, unexpectedly, Darcy takes my hand and brings it toward her arm. My hand is stiff and robotic, and it doesn't feel like a part of me, but Darcy keeps looking into my eyes, and I begin to relax. I let myself go, and my hand gently settles on her skin. Her eyes close, and her mouth goes tight as she breathes in deeply. I start to pull my hand away, but she takes hers and holds it there, and I let her. We stay like that for several long seconds.

"You're the first." She smiles, opening her eyes.

"The first?"

"The first person I've ever let touch my arm."

"It's cool," I say like a total idiot, trying to grab the words back.

"You're cool." Darcy punches my shoulder. "Okay, show's over." She quickly pulls on her long-sleeve shirt and sweater, but her smile remains. "So you're really going to do this?"

"You mean go work the beach?" I ask, surprised at how easily she changed the subject. "Yeah, I have to do this. I have to do it for Gene, I have to do it for the Riptide, for my dad . . ."

"And for you," she adds.

"Yeah, and for me."

Darcy straightens up and takes a deep breath through her nose, making her rosy nostrils flare slightly. "All right, Stretch, you go do what you gotta do. I'll stay here and help your mom get ready."

"Thanks, Darcy." I hoist my bag over my shoulder and head around the side of the house toward my bike. I toss the canvas bag into the metal basket on the front handlebars and swipe my foot at the kickstand.

"Jake!" I turn around and Darcy slams into me, almost knocking me over. She has me in a bear hug. She throws her head back to look up at me. "You're gonna be great out there, you know." She pulls away and wags her finger. "Just don't get hurt."

"Okay." I'm in shock as Darcy reaches up and yanks my head toward hers. She kisses me quickly and runs back to the kitchen door. "Okay."

Wow.

I get on my bike and feel like I could ride the Tour de France.

It's still dark, and the lights on Water Street glow in the morning mist. I'm trying to remember all the things Gene told me about the beach. Where to dig, how much pole he was going to use, when to switch to the mud . . . all that stuff, but my mind keeps drifting back to Darcy Anne Green. *Got to focus.*

"Whoa, watch it!" I look up just in time to swerve my bike out of the way and almost run into a telephone pole. "Geez, Jake, where are you going at this hour?" Johnny Bennato is standing on the sidewalk with a newspaper rolled up under his arm.

"Oh, hey . . . sorry." I wheel my bike back to where he's standing. "I'm going to the beach. Aren't you going to be out there?" I ask, catching my breath.

Johnny squints at his watch. "Man, someone's got you

going out pretty early. Sunrise isn't till five fifty-eight. The DEM is going to be out there real thick, so no one's starting before then." He leans into the telephone pole and scratches his back. "Who're you working for?"

"Nobody. I'm going out there by myself, in Gene's boat." Suddenly I wish I hadn't said that. Doubt is creeping into my mind. I'm starting to feel like this isn't such a good idea after all. I forgot about the DEM being out there. What if they recognize me?

"You going out yourself? In Gene's boat?" Johnny is scratching his head. "Well, I'll be damned. Good for you, Jake, good for you."

"Yeah, it's my first time without Gene, and I got some figuring out to do. His engine is real old and finicky. I usually flood it."

"How's he doing?"

"Not good. He has a bad infection. But he'll pull through."

"Gene's strong; he'll be all right." He slaps me lightly with his rolled-up paper. "You're gonna slay 'em, Jake."

"Thanks, Johnny. Good luck today." I push my bike back out onto the road, and I can hear Johnny whistling to himself as I pedal toward Barrington.

I arrive at Gene's and walk my bike up his shell driveway. His house is dark, and his truck looks lonely as it stares out at the water, like a dog waiting for its owner to come back. The Hawkline sits in the moonlight, tethered to the dock.

I move down the ramp with a wheelbarrow filled with everything I need—gas, lunch, drinking water, a knife, and some tools. The ramp is slippery with the morning mist, and the wheelbarrow almost sends me into the river. I think, *Wow, if I can't get the gas on board safely, how the heck am I going to work for twelve hours at the beach?* I get to the end of the dock and lift the gas and supplies into the old fishing boat.

Jessy is on the bow, staring at me with her yellow beak jutting out and one leg tucked up into her feathers, her other leg still knotted with fishing line.

"Oh, hey, girl. You've been waiting for me?" I see the thick white layer of seagull crap on the bow and realize she's probably been waiting there since Gene got hurt. Broken shells and dead spider crabs litter the deck.

"It's just me today," I say, and start cleaning up the deck. Jessy makes a shrill cry and takes to the air. I watch as she flies off toward Hundred Acre Cove.

It's just me today. Suddenly I'm scared. It's dark and I'm alone and I'm taking Gene's boat without permission and there are going to be a million guys out there and what if I screw up? I'm panicking now.

Gene, tell me it's okay. Tell me it's okay to take your boat.

Let me know it's going to be all right. Promise you're going to be with me out there.

I'm sitting on the gunwale when Jessy comes flying in from the darkness and lands gracefully on the bow with a flutter of wings. She's got something in her beak and drops it on the deck with a loud *thunk.*

A quahog.

That's it. That's the sign. Thank you, Gene. I rinse it off and take out my knife. I slide the blade between the hard outer shells, pressing it into the palm of my hand. It opens easily, and with a gentle twist I expose the soft belly. I loosen the meat from the white-and-purple shell and raise it up to the sky in a toast.

"Here we go," I say to Jessy, and slurp it down in one gulp.

Tossing the shell, I reach for my canvas bag and pull out a small dishtowel. Placing it on my lap, I unwrap it carefully and take out my dad's reading glasses. I'm wondering if my mom will notice the glasses are gone from the top of the register. She's had them there ever since he went missing. I place them carefully on the console, hooking them around a bungee cord that Gene uses to hold his sunglasses and stuff. Once they're in place, I set about getting the boat ready, going through my mental checklist, making sure I'm not forgetting anything.

I attach the gas hose and pump the ball on the gas tank to raise the pressure in the carburetor. The engine whirs and growls — *err, agh, vpp, ttt, zing* — as it starts and spits and tries to fall back to sleep all in the same gasping breath. I'm laughing nervously as this old machine is finding its way back to life, like an old man awakening in the morning. I say a short prayer, and it starts.

I unlash the lines and throw her into gear, and the boat slips from the dock. The green-and-red running light on the bow leads the way through the early morning darkness.

I'm feeling good as I guide the Hawkline up the river and under the bridges, weaving my way slowly through all the sailboats at the yacht club. When I pass the last boat and I'm beyond the red buoy at Blount's Marina, I give the engine enough gas to plane off. I can hear the *swish, swish* sound of the waves slapping at the hull of the boat. She's running well, and I'm early, like I want to be. I make my way past Rumstick Rock and look to the east to see the slightest hint of sunlight fighting its way up to the horizon. I check my watch: 5:08 a.m.

Boats are coming in from all angles now. Dark silhouettes, engines buzzing, make their way through the water toward Barrington Beach. Ronny Camara is running beside me in his seventeen-foot tri-hull. He's looking over at my boat, steering closer, not sure who's at the helm of the Hawkline. When he recognizes me, he pulls away and angles his boat toward Nayatt Point.

I can see the light shining from beneath the flagpole at the Rhode Island Country Club on the distant shoreline. As I get closer, I throttle the old engine down and ease in. As far as the eye can see, boats from everywhere are filling in the area, like a giant jigsaw puzzle. Everyone's moving around, trying to find their spot, and I'm motoring the big Hawkline in between guys from Warwick and Apponaug and East Greenwich. It's tough to see in the first light of the day. I don't know where I'm going, but I'm sure I've arrived. I can't believe how many boats are out here already. There's got to be two thousand boats, and it's not even 5:20 a.m.

I'm looking for a good spot about three hundred yards off the shoreline, right in front of the seventeenth hole of the golf course, just like Gene said. *There!* I see a good-size opening, so I move in slowly.

"Get the hell out of there! That's my spot!"

I look up, and this little muscular guy with red-tinted sunglasses and a bushy mustache is screaming at me. He's cursing and yelling at everybody within fifty yards. I don't want him pissed at me, so I slowly move off ten yards to the west.

"You're good right there, kid," a low voice calls out to

me. I look over to see a tall man with a white beard setting up his rake. He looks Norwegian with his blond hair and strong features. He's working out of a flat-bottomed boat called a garvey. He's motioning with a screwdriver for me to drop anchor.

I toss the anchor, and the boat begins to drift back as I shake the line, helping the hook catch on the bottom. I'm here. I can't believe it; I'm going to work the beach.

It's 5:30 a.m., so I have some time to set up my rake, drink some water, and get some food in me. The man in the garvey is smoking a pipe and pouring hot coffee from a thermos. He's trying to look relaxed, but I can tell he's almost as nervous as I am.

All around me the tension is high as boats jockey for position. The sounds of engines revving and men yelling and dogs barking fill the air. The guy in front of me is Alan Newberry from the West Bay. I know I'm in the right spot if Alan Newberry is on top of me. The guy is a legend on the bullrake. I just hope he doesn't drift back and snag my anchor, sending me adrift into this mess of boats behind me. I'm not sure I can get this old engine started in time to pull me out of that situation.

The light begins to rise over the tree line at Colt State Park, illuminating the bay in oranges and pinks. For the first time, I can see how many boats are out here. They're packed in so tight it's like an enormous raft. I'm not too worried that anyone might hit the Hawkline. She's old and tired and all dinged up; but I just don't want to be the idiot that sets the whole mess into a cluster.

I check the depth of the water with a string and a lead weight. The string has different-colored marks every three feet. I'm embarrassed because all the other guys have electronic depth sounders, but Gene won't spend the money. He always says, "I know every inch of this bay. Don't need any new stuff that's gonna break down and mess up my day." He's right, in a way. The string works just as well and it's practically free. *Tommy would love it.*

The guy in the garvey is watching me. "My dad used to do that when I was a kid. Who taught you that?" Our boats are almost touching now, with the swing of the tide and wind, and he adjusts his anchor line on a series of chocks at the gunwale until his boat shifts away slightly. "Where'd you learn that?" he repeats as I set up the pole and the rake.

"My dad," I say, pulling up the weight and counting the marks. *Ten feet exactly. Just like Gene said.*

I set up my rake and rest it on the gunwale.

"Jake Cole," I say to the Norwegian-looking guy in the next boat.

"What?"

"Jake!" I yell above the outboard motors, banging metal rakes, and barking dogs.

"Cliff Olson. Good to meet you."

Men are readying themselves all around me, preparing their equipment and putting on waterproof aprons. Black Labs and golden retrievers are standing on the bows of boats of all shapes and sizes, barking at one another as pickers are huddled beneath their hooded sweatshirts, awaiting the first haul, deathly afraid to get in the way of their captains. I suddenly realize I'm the captain of this boat right now. It's like the gold rush, and I can't wait to get the rake in the water. I check my watch again.

I still have ten minutes, so I open a can of beef stew and chow down. The stew tastes good, even cold with bits of beef fat congealed and floating in the gravy.

I take a seat on the culling board and survey the boats around me. The little guy with the mustache is still yelling at everyone and chucking things around his boat like a madman so no one will go near him.

Suddenly a cabin boat with two divers on board glides in, and they're about to drop anchor next to the crazy guy. The little guy starts his engine, still swearing, as he backs right up to the stern of the dive boat.

Right about now everyone just wants to start quahogging, but we have to wait until the clam cops blow the horn at 5:58 a.m., so for now we're all watching the little guy get into it with these two divers. Most bull-rakers hate divers because they clean out a spot so good that the quahogs take forever to grow back. This little guy is ready to kill these divers.

He trims his prop up to the waterline and guns the engine, sending a wave of spray into the stern of the dive boat. Then he starts throwing stuff at their cabin. A window breaks on the starboard side and then another. I duck down just enough so I can see and not get busted in the head.

One of the divers heads to the stern and runs right into the spray of water and gets thrown back into his cabin. All the quahoggers are laughing now like it's a comedy show. The other diver sees what's going on and quickly pulls up his anchor, rushing to the controls of his boat.

"Get that piece of crap outta here! *Eels go home, eels go home!*" the little guy chants while waving a machete over his head.

The divers look around to see all of us staring at them, while the clam cops sit outside the pack, looking on like prison guards watching a fight in the jail yard. The captain of the dive boat starts his inboard engines while their pump shoves water out the stern. Diving gear, tanks, masks, and other stuff is floating around in a mess on deck. The tension starts to ease as they move out of the pack and work their way toward shore. The guys all cheer, and the little guy with the mustache returns to his spot, swinging on his anchor, still yelling at everyone around him.

"This is going good," I say to Cliff, who's sitting comfortably on his starboard gunwale.

"Better than expected." He chuckles, with the pipe still tucked in between his teeth.

"And it's not even officially sunrise yet," I say, checking my watch again.

5:56 a.m.

I can feel my pulse thumping in my temples.

21

THE MAIN EVENT

Tuesday morning, August 24

I look over and see one of the clam cops standing up on the bow of his boat as it slowly threads its way through the pack. He's holding an air horn in his hand, and he keeps checking his watch.

Here we go. Any second now I'll be working the beach.

Anchored off to my right, I see Johnny Bennato hustling to set up his bullrake. He's in a perfect spot, right between the crazy little guy and me. I can't believe it. Johnny must have slipped into the pack when that guy was flooding the dive boat. The little guy is so steamed that I don't think he even noticed Bennato. I'm happy that Johnny's beside me.

"Morning, Johnny," I say as he dashes around his boat.

"Jake." He nods, with a sly smile.

One guy, about six boats away from me, throws his rake into the water and starts digging. I look at my watch. It's 5:58 a.m., but the clam cops haven't sounded their horn yet. They speed over and board the guy's boat immediately. Their boat bumps into two others, and soon they're all yelling at one another.

Like thoroughbreds unleashed from the starting gate, four thousand bullrakes hit the water simultaneously, and everyone starts digging. I sit and wait for a minute, listening for the horn, but I'm the only one, so I pull my rake off the holder and throw it in. The guy in the boat that got boarded is standing and pointing as the cop writes out his ticket. The other cop is rifling through his boat, checking for life jackets and stuff. It doesn't seem fair.

My rake hits the bottom with an audible crunch. I try and remember what Gene taught me.

Tickle them out of the hard bottom. Don't force the rake.

At first, the rake seems to just bounce off the bottom, and I really can't figure it out. I look around nervously as guys are pulling up full rakes of littlenecks all around me. I let out some anchor line and push off slightly, trying desperately to get my rake into the bottom. Still not right.

I grab the nut driver off the console, loosen the hose clamp below the handle, and let out another three feet of pole. Instantly the rake seizes up.

I'm in.

I start pulling the rake and quickly realize it's not hard bottom. It's mud. Mud packed so tightly with littlenecks it feels like cement. I close my eyes, trying to block out the craziness around me. I let my mind slowly travel down the length of the pole until I'm sitting right there on the bottom, watching the rake.

Ca-ching, ca-ching.

Less than a minute goes by, and I can hardly move it anymore. I start hauling the pole hand over hand, and I'm amazed at how heavy it is without Gene lifting with me. I try not to let on that I'm struggling. I don't want to look bad in front of all these professional guys.

As the pole rises into the sky, I look behind me, making sure it won't crack someone in the head when it comes down. I carefully angle the pole so it splashes down into the water between two boats.

I look back into the rake and can't believe my eyes. It's jammed full of the prettiest quahogs I've ever seen. There's got to be over a hundred littlenecks in there, all of them the perfect size. I shake the rake to release the mud and dump the catch onto the culling board with a loud rattle.

"Doesn't get any better than this." Johnny Bennato smiles as he pulls on his rake handle.

"Unbelievable," I say, throwing my rake back into the water.

Just then this guy they call Mickey the Pimp forgets to look behind him, and his pole and handle come smashing down on my starboard gunwale about six inches from my head.

"You stupid bastard, get off the beach if you can't work the crowds! You almost clocked my kid!" Johnny yells at him at the top of his lungs.

The guy grunts and moves his pole to rest in the water, off the bow of the Hawkline.

I ignore Mickey's grumblings because he's trying to blame me, and I just focus on the work. The conditions are just right. I'm making the rake head sing, but it's getting harder and harder to pull this thing up to the surface. I figure at this rate I won't last till noon. Guys are crossing over one another with their poles; handles are getting locked together; it's a circus out here. My rake hits the surface again and again, and each time it's filled to the teeth. I start counting and figuring in my head. I'm thinking I might be able to catch enough today to make a huge dent into that debt we owe Vito.

Just focus on the work.

When I hit the second hour, I decide to put on a pair of cotton gloves. I'm hoping they'll help me last a little longer out here and keep my hands free of blisters. I dip the gloves in the warm August water, wiggle them onto my hands, and continue pulling the rake. I work quickly, using my shoulders, leaning back and putting all one hundred and seventy pounds of my weight into the rake. It happens over and over again, and it seems there's no end to the quahogs.

After two hours I've already got eight bags on board, about four thousand littlenecks. Before the beach opened, we were getting twenty cents apiece, so I figure I'm making about eight hundred dollars per hour. If I can work ten hours, I'll make eight thousand dollars. Wow!

Hold it. Stop thinking like that. I catch myself again.

My head is down, and I'm working the rake, and the ache in my back feels like a sawtooth steak knife being driven between my shoulder blades. The gloves keep getting bunched up, and they are digging their way into my knuckles, so I ditch them. The blisters are coming.

It's 9:30 a.m., and I'm already tired. I tie the rake off and sit down on the gunwale and hurriedly pick through the catch on the culling board until it's covered only with littlenecks. I wish I didn't have to keep stopping to sort through everything, count it, and put them into bags. Maybe I should have taken Darcy out here with me. I think of her back at the diner, probably rushing between booths and tables, prepping for the lunch crowd. She's definitely a distraction, but a nice one. I throw the rake back in, and I see somebody paddling out in a bright-orange kayak.

Uh-oh, this isn't going to be good.

I'm thinking that this crazy fool is going to try and bull-rake out of his kayak. As he gets closer, I can see it's a kid. Probably out looking for his dad or selling jugs of water or something. I get back to work, but I keep one eye on the orange kayak. The kid has his binoculars out, scanning the horizon. The next thing I know, he's paddling right toward me.

It's Tommy!

I'd give him a wave, but the other guys are all laughing at him and making jokes.

"No-wake zone, man. Don't make any waves," one guy shouts.

"You lost? Newport Beach is twelve miles south of here." Another points toward Prudence Island. The quahoggers are heckling him as he circumnavigates the pack of boats.

I lift my hat and give him a half wave as I wipe my brow with my arm, trying to make it look like I'm not waving at all. Tommy slides in front and drifts down on me, paddling to stay in my path.

"Hey, Jake, I found you!"

"Get in the boat. Can't you see I'm working here?" I yell at him.

"I'm just out here to help. Chill out."

"Come on, get on board." I lift him up by the arm, and we pull the kayak up and lash it to the bow of the Hawkline. When that's done, I start working the rake again, and Tommy sits on the rail looking at me like, *What'd I do?*

"These guys are all staring at me already, so I'm a little self-conscious. That orange kayak got them all laughing at you, and I guess they're laughing at me too, that's all."

"What do you care what those other guys think?" Tommy looks around at the pack of boats surrounding us.

Tommy is right. I actually don't care what these other guys think. "Yeah, you're right. Sorry."

Then Tommy starts looking at all the quahogs in the boat. "Holy crap. Did you catch all these?"

"They didn't just jump in the boat. Are you sticking around? I could use the help . . . and the company."

"I'm in as long as you need me," he says, slapping his hands together and giving me a *Where do we start?* look.

"We've got a long day ahead of us, and I'll make it worth your while."

"I'm not doing it for the money, Jake," Tommy says, waving me off. "This'll be fun. What do I do?"

I'm relieved that Tommy's going to stay. It gives me new energy.

"Okay. When I say *Ready up,* grab that rope and haul it in as I pull up the pole, until the rake comes up to the surface."

"Got it," Tommy says, getting into position.

"Ready up!"

Tommy grabs the rope and starts hauling.

"Toooooo fast! Slow down!"

The rake busts the surface, and the pole is nearly bent in half from the pressure of the line.

"Come on, Tommy! You're gonna break my poles."

"Geez, man, just tell me. Don't get so touchy." Tommy looks like a beaten dog with his head hanging low as the other quahoggers look on.

"When you are out here working in this boat, I'm in charge, so you got to listen to everything I tell you and don't take it personally. Everything has to go right out here, or stuff gets broken and people get hurt. My track record sucks with people getting hurt."

"I know. So, just tell me what to do and I'll do it . . . Captain." Tommy gives me an exaggerated salute.

"Don't call me that," I say, thinking of George. I dump the rake onto the culling board. "First thing is to get rid of anything that's not a quahog, and pull out the undersize quahogs." I hand him the set of steel rings and point to the smallest one. "If any of them fit through that, throw 'em overboard because they're undersize.

Anything else that fits through this bigger one goes into this bucket."

"Tiny ones overboard; everything else in the bucket. Got it."

"But you got to count them too. When you get five hundred in the bucket, you got to bag them."

"Where do these big ones go?" Tommy asks, holding up one of the large chowders.

"Just put them in the red bucket. We don't need to count those."

I kick one of the full white buckets. "This one's ready to be bagged. Just lay one of those red onion bags across the lip and flip it with your wrists."

"Like this?" Tommy flips the bucket and the littlenecks rattle into the bag.

"Yeah, like that. Cool. No one ever gets the first one! Great!"

Tommy looks over his shoulder, pleased with himself.

"You're now officially a picker, Tommy. You know the only thing that's lower than a picker?"

Tommy is not looking up; he's just shoveling quahogs, moving rocks. He says, "No, Jake, what's lower than a picker?"

"A snot."

I'm laughing so hard I can barely pull the rake.
This is fun. It hurts, but it's fun.

22

A HELPING HAND

Tuesday morning, August 24

Out of the corner of my eye, I see a brand-new boat slinking through the pack, searching for a space to drop anchor. The guy steering the boat is about twenty years old, pudgy, hair slicked back with gel, and he's wearing a bright-blue tank top. I watch him as he dumps his anchor to the port side of me. His boat is clean, without a speck of mud on it, and it looks like he just launched it for the first time today. He lets out his line and settles in right next to us. Our boats are nearly touching, and he's no more than ten feet from Cliff Olson's garvey. Cliff doesn't say anything about him invading our space, so I don't either.

The pudgy guy glances over at me as he's setting up his rake. He's doing it exactly backward, attaching his rake first and then trying to hold on to it as he attaches the other sections of pole. His face gets red with strain as he tries to set up. He's swearing and muttering as he struggles.

"Check it out. Trust Fund Guy is going to dig with the rest of us today," Tommy whispers to me.

"He looks like he needs some help."

Just as I say this, the guy drops both his pole and rake into the water. In a split second he loses two hundred bucks' worth of equipment, and it looks like he's never dug a quahog in his life. He might not get the chance today.

The guy starts stomping around the boat, throwing his screwdriver against the console, shattering a full bottle of beer in the fancy cup holder. Then he throws another section of pole onto the deck, and it makes a metallic, clattering noise that startles the rest of the diggers. He slumps down on the gunwale, looking completely dejected. I know how he feels. I've totally been there.

"Tommy, come hold the rake for a minute."

"You want me to dig?"

"No, don't pull it or you'll mess it up. It's half full." I jump onto the bow and pull out a set of scuba fins, mask, and fifty feet of coiled rope from the storage hold.

"What are you doing?"

"I'll be right back," I say.

The pudgy guy's boat is so close it's almost touching ours. I get his attention by clearing my throat loudly.

"Can I come aboard?" I ask.

"Sure, but I don't know what you're gonna do. I just lost the friggin' rake, pole, and clamps. All gone!"

"I know. I saw it happen. The good thing is you're on an anchor, and you haven't moved, so it's probably right under us," I say, jumping aboard his boat. I take a look around, and this guy is set up. Everything looks like it just got unwrapped from the store: new poles, perfectly clean rubber deck mats, pristine white fiberglass culling board, even the buckets are new. *Who the hell buys their buckets?* I ask myself.

"So what're you gonna do? Dive for it?" he asks, eyes wide.

"Yeah. Unless you're going to do it," I say, holding the fins out to him.

"Dude, I can't even swim," he says, shaking his head.

"It's settled, then. But we got to be quick. Those boats are drifting back on us, and they're not going to be too happy with us just sitting here." I nod toward the two boats in front of us about twenty yards away.

Stripping down to my underwear, I put on the fins, tie a snap hook to one end of the rope, and hand the other end to the guy.

"What do I do with this?"

"Just hold on to it. I'm going to hook the other end to your rake," I say, snapping the hook.

"Why are you doing this for me? I don't even know your name."

"I don't know. I guess I just know what it's like to be stuck in a bad situation," I say, looping the rope around my waist and stepping over the side. "My name's Jake Cole."

"I'm Paul," the guy says quietly, almost embarrassed.

"Okay, wish me luck."

I jump in the water and take a couple of huge breaths as I try to determine where the rake might be in relation to the boat.

Right under me.

I dive straight down into the dark. The sound of outboard motors and the clanging of poles against boats is a dull roar in my head. Fifteen feet down, my hands hit the muddy bottom, and I pinch my nose and blow out to relieve the pressure. My ears pop with a loud squeak, and immediately I begin to sweep my hands across the surface of the mud, searching for Paul's rake. I can feel the quahogs all clustered together right under the surface, and part of me wants to start picking them up. *Keep searching. You're running out of air.* My lungs are burning, and there is a convulsive tug in the middle of my chest that is telling me to get to the surface. I take one more sweep with my hands and feel nothing. I kick hard toward the surface.

"Holy crap. You were down there for like an hour! How'd you do that?" Paul is leaning over the rail, looking pale and worried.

"My dad," I say, panting, "would get me to swim underwater . . . retrieve things under the dock . . . I just got used to it, that's all."

"Yeah, my dad makes me retrieve things too," Paul says with a curious smile.

"I can't see a thing down there."

"It's no use, man. I'll just head in," Paul says, slapping the side of the boat. "My dad is going to kill me. He just bought all this stuff for me last week. Said it would be good for me to earn a hard day's pay. This sucks."

"I'm not through trying. I can get it." I look over at Tommy. "How we doing? Those boats getting close?"

"You'd better hurry up," Tommy says nervously. "They're starting to give me some nasty looks."

I head back down, popping my ears on the way. This time I find the section of pole on my first sweep. *Bingo*. I feel my way down the pole till I find the rake and grab it with my left hand, using my right hand to unhook the rope around my waist. I snap the hook onto the rake and begin my ascent.

Suddenly, everything goes wrong. A sharp web of rope

hits me, and I spin around, twisting through the murky water. There's a sudden tug on my leg as it wraps me in its noose and pulls me back down, dragging me across the bottom. I frantically pull and tear at the rope around my leg, kicking the fins off as my breath leaves me in a flurry of bubbles.

I've got to free myself.

All I want to do is breathe.

I can't breathe.

I can't breathe.

I don't want to die, I don't want to die.

I feel two hands lift me up, and then I see a flash of knife slicing through the murk, and then lots of bubbles as the hands push me up toward the light. My head bursts through the surface, and I suck in air with a roaring noise. Cliff Olson pops up next to me, with the knife still in his hand.

"Jake! Jake!" Tommy is screaming at me from the boat. "What happened?" He lifts me into the boat with some newfound power I didn't know he had.

"I'm all right," I gasp, dropping the mask to the deck. "I just got caught up in some guy's drifting anchor line."

I look over and see Cliff climbing back into his garvey, like he does this kind of thing every day. Paul jumps over into the Hawkline with a towel and my clothes.

"Jesus Christ, that was some crazy stuff! You nearly

got yourself killed." He is visibly shaking, and his eyes look like they are going to pop out of his head. "I thought you were just playing a joke like you were some kind of Harry Houdini, until this dude comes jumping across the two boats and dives in with a knife between his teeth."

We all look at Cliff, and he's already back on his rake and pulling in a steady rhythm. "Hey, Cliff!" I yell over to him.

"Yeah, Jake?"

"Thanks. I owe you," I say, still panting like a dog.

"Don't worry about it, Jake." He points to a red boat about fifty feet away, where another digger is hauling up his anchor line. "That guy was dragging his anchor because it was caught up in a bunch of old eel traps. I guess I cut you both free."

"Well, then, *he* owes you." Tommy laughs, pointing to the guy in the red boat.

Cliff and I are nervously laughing it off, but Paul looks pretty freaked out.

"Did you pull up the rope?" I ask, smiling at Paul.

"What?"

"Your rake, did you pull it up?"

"No way." He rubs his face with his fat fingers like he can't believe it. "You clipped it?"

"Yeah. But this time," I say, "start putting it together

from the handle end first. Put the rake on last, and make sure you tie a damn line to the end of it because I'm not diving in after it again."

"You're un-freakin'-believable," he says, pulling his wallet out of his back pocket and grabbing a wad of bills. He holds the money out toward me.

"Seriously, don't worry about it," I say, handing him the towel.

"Unbelievable," he says again as he jumps back into his shiny new boat.

Tommy and I get back to work, and I can still hear Paul muttering to himself. I thought I would be exhausted after nearly drowning, but for some reason I feel even stronger.

"Why did you help that guy?" Tommy asks me while dumping another bucket of littlenecks into a bag.

"Because he needed it, I guess."

"But the guy is clueless," Tommy says under his breath.

"Hey, you were clueless when you first paddled out here in that kayak."

"Yeah, that's true," Tommy says, nodding.

"Sometimes you gotta do what you gotta do."

23

TACTICAL MOVES

Tuesday, August 24

By 11:30 a.m. the rakes are no longer coming up full. I move up on the anchor line because there's nowhere to move behind me.

"Are you still catching?" I ask Johnny Bennato.

"Seems everybody's coming up with about half of what they were catching an hour ago," he says.

"Me too."

"Say, you all right?" Johnny asks. "I heard you ran into a little trouble over there. I was so busy dealing with these bozos in front of me, I didn't even see it."

"Yeah, I'm fine."

"We're awesome!" Tommy adds, throwing his skinny arm over the console.

Bennato's pushing the handle of his rake forward with his hips, just like me, really sweating to make the rake work, and he's pissed off as he starts pulling it up to the surface. "Friggin' bottom's all chewed up. There seems to be plenty of stuff, but it's like working in a newly plowed cornfield. The rake keeps popping out."

The wind from the north has died, and there's no tide. All the boats are starting to drift around at different angles.

"The tide should be going out for another hour." I say this to nobody in particular.

Tommy has caught up with me, and he has everything culled out, and all the buckets are bagged and stacked. Not a good sign.

"I'm thinking of moving," I say real quietly.

"What?" Tommy looks at me like I'm nuts. "Where are we going to go? There are boats everywhere."

"East of here. There's no one working over there." I nod with my chin toward Rumstick Rock.

"Don't you think there's a reason no one's working over there?"

"Listen." I lean in close to Tommy. "The wind is going to pick up any minute, and we'll try working that mud drift out there."

"Wind?" Tommy licks his finger and holds it up into the stagnant air.

"Trust me, it's going to blow, and all these guys are going to end up in a tangled mess."

"You're the boss," Tommy says.

As I look back at the mountain of quahogs we've caught, I don't feel like a kid anymore. I feel like I'm a Hi-Liner, like Dave Becker. Gene would be proud of me. So would my dad.

"Let's just pull up to the top of our anchor line and eat some lunch."

"Sounds good to me. I'm starving." Tommy pulls most of the anchor line in as I rinse my hands in the water. The salt stings my palms. There are three burst blisters on each hand. The skin is hanging off in little flaps, and I try to press them back into place, but it's useless, so I just bite off the extra skin and spit it overboard.

"I hope you got more for lunch than that," Tommy says, leaning into the anchor line.

"Nope, that's it," I say, offering him my hand. If Tommy weren't here, I might have gone home by now.

We tie off, and I hand Tommy a loaf of bread and open the other can of beef stew. We eat as if we are starving, scarfing down the bread and stew without taking time to breathe.

"Gene always says that August is the only time when you can really predict the weather out here. The mornings are cool with little wind, and then in the afternoon you get a warm southerly breeze." I hand the jug of water to Tommy. "That's what we're waiting for, so let me know when you feel it."

"Yeah, right." Tommy laughs. "I can't feel anything. My arms are blasted."

As his words empty into the air, a southerly breeze comes, slight at first, just a tickle on the back of my neck. It's as if Gene is right here with me.

"Haul the anchor, Tom. Haul it fast."

I smack the rake into the rake holder and resurrect the engine. The smoke and noise from the engine arouses everyone's attention. I can hear a guy from Greenwich Bay in a light-green boat talking loudly.

"It's about time this place clears out of all these kids and peckerheads."

"Hey dick-for-brains," Bennato yells at him. "My money would be on the kid. He's outcaught you, you jackass."

The Greenwich Bay guy starts throwing his rake around and smashing stuff on his deck. I decide to swing the boat by Johnny Bennato, when I notice Tommy stacking the bags in a big mound to show off our catch.

"Don't do that. Lay them out flat," I call back to him.

"Why? It looks wicked awesome."

"We're not here to show off. Just get them down low."

Tommy reluctantly pulls the bags down and lays them in two rows of ten bags each at the stern.

"Where are you going, Jake?" Johnny asks over the engine noise.

I kill the engine and slide right by his starboard side, speaking in a hushed voice.

"I'm setting up for the mud drift out east of here because the wind is going to blow this afternoon from the south. Gene and I killed them in the mud one foggy day near the line out east. I figure it'll be even better than here."

Johnny hauls up his half-full rake. "I'll see you out there."

A few guys like C. J. and Becker are on the move too. I can see the guys in the pack getting all tangled up with the freshening breeze. Johnny leans over his rail so I can hear him better and says quietly, "A lot of these guys can't work in the mud. They'll be going home soon."

I slowly navigate my way out of the pack, with Johnny following me. I see that Cliff Olson is also pulling up his anchor now.

"We are going to mow 'em now, Tommy, you watch."

I pull the boat due south, almost even with Rumstick Rock, and kill the engine. I take the hard-bottom rake off the end of the pole and put on Gene's mud rake. It looks huge with its wide basket and three-and-a-half-inch teeth. I'm wondering if I can even pull this big rake when the wind picks up.

The wind and the waves start to build. I can see guys leaving with loaded boats. The sound of a thousand straining engines screaming with effort fills the air. To the west of us a cloud of smoke rises from a boat that is on fire near the lighthouse. I can see the fire department rushing to launch their boat at the ramp on Barrington Beach.

"You feel that wind now, Tommy? It won't be long before all their anchors will start failing. You'll see a cluster of boats snarled together in ten minutes."

"Glad we're out here, then," Tommy says, looking around. There are only a handful of boats working this area. I throw the rake in and move toward the bow so the boat will cut through the waves. I just manage to hold on. Waves slap the side of the boat, and the rake is singing along, *tick, tick, tick,* as the quahogs find their way in.

"Ready up!"

The line strains from the bigger rake, and Tommy is helping me more and more as the day wears on. The rake hits the surface, bouncing in the chop, and it's jammed to the teeth with littlenecks.

"Wow! You *are* amazing," Tommy says as the quahogs hit the culling board.

"Keep telling me that, because I don't know how much longer I can hang on. My hands are a mess."

The Hawkline is riding low. I can feel the momentum of the overloaded boat slam into each wave as we head south, getting ready for another mile-long drift. All afternoon, boats pass us heading home, looking at us like we're crazy. Little do they know we're catching four bags each drift.

I'm working directly off of the bow now, quartering into the waves and leaning back. My shoulders no longer just hurt; they ache from the strain. The sun is getting lower in the late August burn that leaves the western sky almost pink.

"Let's take a swim."

"Sounds good to me," Tommy says, rinsing his hands over the side.

The boat is drifting north toward the beach, so I set up the anchor off the bow, and it catches in the mud. All the people who were standing on the beach, gawking at us quahoggers, have gone home.

I start to strip down.

"You going in naked?" Tommy asks, looking at all the houses right up against the shore.

"Yeah, I'm too tired to care, and I don't want to spend the rest of the evening working in wet underwear." I hang my clothes off the steering wheel and jump in. Tommy follows my lead.

We've got the radio blaring, and Tommy is singing along as he swims on his back. I swim around behind the old engine and look at it from the waterline. It's a greasy mess with oil and smoky soot all over it. I am amazed at how it still starts up each time. I continue to swim around to the east side of the boat, inspecting the hull.

"Look at the boat, Tom. She's down below the water-line, full of quahogs. I've never seen her so low."

Tommy swims around to my side.

"We have a problem."

"It's no problem. We'll just take it slow, that's all." I say this, still looking at the underside of the gunwale. Tommy grabs my shoulder.

"No, we have a real problem." He's whispering now. "Jay Miller is drifting by on the other side of our boat."

"So what?"

"Janna is on board, picking for him," Tommy says, wide-eyed.

"Perfect. Now's your chance, Tommy." I laugh. "You should swim over and say hi."

"What are we going to do?" Tommy looks worried.

I peek around the bow and see her from the back. She's beautiful from every angle, with her long legs and blond hair. I start giggling uncontrollably at our situation. We're both hiding behind the Hawkline and watching her prance around the boat in her bikini.

"We can't swim forever. Let's just quickly hoist up onto the port side and get our clothes on while she's working," I suggest.

I swim up and make the first move to get on board, swinging my leg over the rail. I fall to the deck and lie there for a second.

"Is the coast clear?" Tommy whispers from the side of the boat.

"Yeah. They're not looking, come on."

I hear Tommy struggling, trying to get in, and it sounds like he's banging himself up pretty good on the side of the boat.

"I need a hand," he yells out. I look over, and Janna has her back to us. Jay is huddled under his console, trying to light his pipe. I quickly jump to my feet and reach over the rail and grab Tommy's wrists and pull.

"Come on, kick!" I'm ordering, and Tommy is kicking, but I just start laughing, and all the strength drains out of me again. I can't help him at all. I reach over with both arms under his armpits and use my knees to pull him over the rail.

When I turn, Jay's looking at us, and he motions to Janna. There we are, both naked as can be. They can't be more than twenty yards away, just staring. Tommy shrieks and we both hit the deck, and I can hear Janna laughing with her father.

Tommy dries off with this rank towel that's been in the boat since the beginning of the summer. It smells so much like mold that I decide to just sit on the cooler box and dry off in the late afternoon sun. The Millers' boat is well behind us now, and I can see Janna still looking up once in a while to check us out.

"I think she's just as curious about us as we are about her," I say.

"Dude, I think you mean curious about me." Tommy is still scrambling to get his clothes on.

"Whatever." My mind drifts back to this morning and the kiss from Darcy. I can still feel it. "You know, Darcy kissed me good luck this morning."

"*Kiss* kissed you?" Tommy is looking at me with his jaw hanging open.

"Yeah. I'm not sure if it was a good-luck kiss, but I'm pretty sure she likes me."

"Darcy?" Tommy is still dumbfounded.

"Yeah, Darcy. What's wrong with Darce?"

"Nothing." Tommy is scratching his head. "No, she's awesome. I just never thought . . ."

"I know. It was kind of unexpected, but I really dig her."

"That's cool." Tommy starts pulling the anchor line as I get dressed, and I can tell the conversation is over. Time to get back to work.

Suddenly Jay Miller's boat pulls up right alongside ours.

"You guys okay?" Jay yells over.

"Yeah. We're good."

"Good, 'cause I thought I saw two naked guys climbing into your boat." Jay's laughing, and Janna slaps him on the arm. "Thought you might have been stowing refugees."

"Just quahogs," I call back, a little red in the face.

Tommy lifts the rake from the rail, tosses it into the wave, and begins pulling the rake to show off, but the poor guy doesn't know what he is doing. He's just mimicking what I do, and it's funny. Jay Miller is laughing out loud as Tommy is doing the herky-jerky all over the place like a comedian. Janna is laughing and I'm cracking up too. Tommy starts putting on a show, making faces, and pretending he's me by standing on a bucket while he's raking. I think Janna is checking him out.

The sun is painting the bay, and everything in it, with a warm amber glow. There are only a couple hundred guys still out here working, and only five or six boats where we are. I take the rake from Tommy and fill it with quahogs for him when Janna's not looking. Then I let him pull it to the surface. He must be working on adrenaline combined with passion, because he breaks that rake out of the mud and snakes it up to the surface like Gene himself. Janna claps as the full rake comes to the surface, and Tommy bows like he's onstage. Tommy can't stop looking over at Jay's boat. I can't blame him.

• • •

My body is numb. I'm exhausted and hungry and my hands are raw and bleeding, and part of me wants to head in, but I know I can't. Not yet. I can still catch more.

I look toward Rumstick Rock and see Tommy's dad bashing toward us in their small Whaler. He's got the engine punched, and I can hear it winding out as he bounces across the waves. He pulls up on us fast.

"Your dad's here, Tommy!"

Tommy stands up, smiling, happy to see him. "Yeah, I called him at work before I came out here, and he said he'd go to the diner to get us some food if he got off early enough."

"Wow, that's cool. I can't believe he found us. So wait a minute, you planned to help me all along, didn't you?"

"Of course. You think I'm going to let you have all the fun?"

I wave to Tommy's dad as his boat settles right next to us. "Hey, Mr. Clancy."

He doesn't answer. He's just staring at the pile of quahogs on board, his mouth wide open. "My God, that's a lot of littlenecks. Did you catch all these?"

"They didn't just jump into the boat," Tommy says, smiling at me.

Mr. Clancy climbs aboard, carrying two shopping bags stained with grease.

"Thanks, Mr. Clancy. This is great." I look into one

of the bags, and it's got everything: burgers, fries, fried chicken, and lots of ketchup.

We start chowing down, and Mr. Clancy notices Tommy glancing over at the Millers' boat.

"Who are your friends?" Before Tommy or I can stop him, he stands up and calls out to them, "You want some food? We have plenty!"

"Daaad!" Tommy is embarrassed.

"What? We do," he says, hefting the other bag. I can see Jay talking with Janna, and she's nodding. Jay stows his rake and moves to the console.

"They're coming over. . . ." I tease Tommy.

"Great. Thanks, Dad."

Mr. Clancy takes another look at Jay's boat and sees Janna, and suddenly he smiles and slaps Tommy on the back.

The Millers' boat approaches, and we lash all the boats together like a raft.

"What a day, huh, Jake?" Jay smiles at me. "You know my daughter, Janna, right? Janna, this is Jake. I used to work with his dad."

"Hi," I say, with a mouth full of burger.

"I'm Tommy." Tommy's voice cracks.

"Hi." Janna *sounds* like a mermaid too.

Mr. Clancy shakes Jay's hand, and the two of them

crack open beers and get into a discussion about fishing. The three of us climb onto the bow and I dole out the food.

"You guys are good at this," Janna says, inspecting our catch. "I think you almost have as much as my dad."

"We got lucky, I guess," I say.

"My dad said that you're gonna be a great fisherman."

"I don't want to be a fisherman." I'm surprised at myself for saying it, but it's true.

"You don't? Why are you out here, then?"

"The money's good and we need money," I say, biting into my second burger.

"What do you guys need money for?"

"I don't need money." Tommy points at me with a drumstick. "Jake needs money."

"I'm trying to save the diner where me and my mom live," I explain.

I say this knowing I left out a lifetime's worth of stuff in between, but I figure she doesn't want to hear about my dad going missing, the loan from the Mafia, and everything else, so I just come out and ask her if she wants to come to the cabaret tomorrow night.

"The what?" Janna looks puzzled.

"A cabaret," Tommy says. "You know . . . music, dancing, food? It's for a good cause."

I'm surprised because Janna jumps to her feet and bounces over to her dad. "Jake and his mom are having a cabaret tomorrow night. . . . Can we go?"

Jay takes the pipe from his mouth. "Tomorrow?"

"Yeah, they're trying to raise money to save their diner."

"It's at seven. Right in town on Water Street, near Blount Seafood," I add.

"I know where it is, Jake." Jay puts his arm around Janna. "I thought you were going with your girlfriends to the movies."

"I can go with them on Saturday. Please?" Janna takes a fistful of Jay's shirt in her hand in a pretend threat.

Jay turns to me and says, "Yeah, we'll be there."

Janna smiles at Tommy, and he nearly falls out of the boat.

Jay knocks his pipe clean on the side of the boat and stuffs it into his shirt pocket. "Well, we got to get back to work." He shakes Mr. Clancy's hand and steps into his boat. "Janna?"

"I'm staying with the boys."

"No, you're not."

"I'm joking, Dad." She hops on board like a gazelle.

"I'm in love," Tommy whispers.

24
SELLING OUT
Tuesday evening, August 24

Tommy's dad anchors his Whaler and comes back on board to help us out. I begin pulling the rake, and he's stacking bags, tidying the boat, cleaning the bow area, and pulling seaweed from the deck.

"Keep that up, Dad, and you'll put me out of a job," Tommy says.

"Me too," I say.

Mr. Clancy just laughs and keeps on working.

The last hour turns out to be the best of the day, as the wind slows down just right, and we add another five bags of littlenecks to the pile.

"Forty bags of littlenecks and eight bags of chowders," Mr. Clancy announces, slapping his hand down on the huge pile. "I can't imagine what that's worth."

"A lot," Tommy says, reaching up to give me a high five. I stick out my elbow and he slaps it.

Mr. Clancy looks at Tommy, and he's leaning against the railing with barely the energy to stand.

"I'd better get you and your kayak back home."

"I'm not leaving, Dad. Jake needs me, even if it's to haul this stuff up the dock."

"I guess your mother will understand. You guys going to be all right getting in?"

"Yeah, we'll take it slow. Last couple of rakes, and then we'll be in right behind you," I say reassuringly, throwing the rake up on the holder and starting the engine. It coughs and spits back to life.

"Gene's outboard sounds as tired as you are right now," Mr. Clancy says.

We load Tommy's kayak onto the Whaler, and Mr. Clancy climbs aboard. "We'll see you at home, Tommy. Good luck selling out. Hope you get a good price."

"Okay, Dad," Tommy says. I hear that word *Dad* and I start to feel it inside. *Look at me, Dad, with forty-eight bags of quahogs on board. Look at me today, Dad. Look at what I did today.*

Twenty minutes later the sun starts to settle on the horizon as I dismantle the rake and pole. Tommy begins rearranging the bags around the boat to even out the weight. Just off our bow I can see Cliff in his garvey, heading toward us. His gray boat is heaped with red bags.

"How'd you hit 'em, Jake?"

"Hey, Cliff." I sit down on the gunwale.

"Oh, my God, you crushed them today. Christ, you must have fifty bags."

"Forty-eight with the chowders. Isn't everyone catching forty-eight bags?" Tommy says, pretending to sound naive.

"Not everyone." He laughs. "How old are you, anyway?" he asks, looking over my gear.

"Fourteen."

"Me too," Tommy adds proudly.

"Fourteen years old and you're catching forty-eight bags—that's gotta be a record." Cliff is shaking his head. "Only in Rhode Island."

"Where are *you* from?"

Cliff mumbles something under his breath.

"Where?" I ask.

"Well, there's no point in lying to a kid, probably a kid without a license, right?"

"No, I have a license. Gene always buys a license for me in case we catch over our limit."

"I'm from Patchogue, Long Island."

"Long Island . . . cool. How'd you get here? Did you take your boat here?" Tommy asks.

"No, I trailered up. I've been here all summer."

"I haven't seen you out here before."

"I've seen you in this Hawkline before. You were with someone else, working that mud drift out east of Prudence, right before the hurricane."

You can hear Tommy groaning as he lifts the last white bucket and flips it into the red onion bag. He looks like he's going to collapse any second.

"Is your picker okay?"

"No," Tommy blurts out, holding his back.

"We are both hurting actually, but we'll be okay in a few days."

"Sorry to hear that. What's your full name, Jake? I know you told me earlier, but I couldn't hear you with the noise and all."

"Jake Cole, and this is Tommy Clancy."

"Well, Mr. Jake Cole and Tommy Clancy, I'll follow you into the dock because you're riding kinda low, not much freeboard there in that old Hawkline. Are you selling out at Easton's? That's where my truck and trailer are."

Selling out. I've been so busy trying to catch the quahogs, I haven't thought where I would be selling them. Gene usually sells out at Gilbert's, but it's a long haul from the dock to his place. At Easton's you can tie up right next to the scales.

The old engine starts up and grinds into gear as I move

the throttle forward slowly. Cliff is behind me, sitting in my wake a hundred yards back. I can feel the setting sun over my shoulders as I make the turn around Rumstick Rock and head into the Warren River.

I can see the lights from the parking lot at Easton's Seafood. There are a few red-faced quahoggers standing around a cooler, laughing and drinking beer. I see Bainesy pissing against the seawall as I kill the engine and slide into the dock space. Tommy lashes the bowline. I grab the stern line and pull us in tight. The guys standing by their trucks continue drinking and telling jokes. I think they're laughing at Tommy and me at first, but after a minute I realize they're all just happy because they have a pocket full of money now.

I start to load the bags onto the edge of the dock, stacking them flat so they won't fall over into the water. I have two rows of ten bags each on the bottom. I start working on the second row. One guy, Michael Stanzione, comes over to look at our catch.

"Hey, Toad," he calls out to this buddy, who they call Toad because his name is Todd and he's always licking his lips. Toad ignores him and continues drinking and telling stories. Tommy and I are just stacking bag after bag on the dock, pretending we're not seeing or hearing any of this. I'm stacking slowly because my hands are a mess.

"Toad, come down here and check out Jake's catch."
A few of the quahoggers stop talking and begin making
their way over to the dock. One of the men counts the
bags with his index finger.

"Stop counting, you ass. The kid caught forty-eight
bags. I already counted them!" Michael shouts.

"You catch all these quahogs by yourself?" Toad asks.

They're staring at Cliff, who is idling his boat just off-
shore, as if he's wary of all these guys being around. Cliff
has a tarp out, and he's covering all his quahogs.

"I had Tommy picking for me most of the day."
Tommy keeps cleaning the boat, never looking up,
but he's laughing under his breath. He still must have a
hard time thinking of me as his captain and of himself as
my picker.

"Everybody had a picker today," Toad says.

The rest of the guys, including Bainsey, come down
to look.

Without my even asking them, the guys all start
helping us out, moving up the dock with two bags each.
Billy Mac pretends he's putting two bags in the back of his
pickup truck to get a rise out of me. By the time Tommy
and I get the last two bags onto the dock, these guys have
the rest all stacked outside the garage door.

"Tommy, stay here with the boat while I go sell out."

"Yes, sir!" Tommy says sarcastically.

"Thanks!" I yell as the quahoggers move up the street toward Jack's Bar.

"Let's go to Tweets for a pound of red and a pound of white pasta," I hear Billy Mac bark as they round the corner toward the bar.

I take a big breath as Cliff Olson, my new Long Island friend, slides in past the Hawkline.

"I thought they'd never leave," Cliff says.

The garvey grinds hard on the shell boat ramp. I wonder if it's stuck. Cliff backs off with the engine and comes in ever so slowly this time.

"Need some help?" I ask him.

"No, I'm good."

Cliff's boat is up and out of the water in seconds. It's a thing of beauty. He parks his trailer and boat, then walks together with me to Easton's Seafood. Russell, the quahog buyer, comes out of his office and looks over the stack of quahogs resting at his door.

"What's the price, Russell?" Cliff asks.

"Ten cents apiece, take it or leave it," Russell says, rolling up the sleeves of his flannel shirt.

"Are you kidding me? The price was twenty-two cents apiece just yesterday, and you want to give the kid ten cents. Let's take 'em somewhere else, Jake. I'll get the truck." Cliff starts walking back to his rig.

"Suit yourself, but no one else is going to take fifty

bags off your hands at this hour. Not today," Russell says. "Hell, I got more quahogs than I can get rid of. These things are going to rot before I can ship 'em out."

The ground beneath me starts to fall away, and I get dizzy. I feel like Santiago in *The Old Man and the Sea*, when he finally gets home and his marlin is only a carcass.

"You're Jake Cole, right? You used to work for Gene?" Russell asks as soon as Cliff is out of earshot.

"Yes. Gene got hurt a couple weeks back. Couldn't work today," I say in a trance. Russell starts scribbling on his notepad and tears off a sheet, handing it to me. I turn it over in my hand and it reads:

.13 cents apiece (John Cole)

"Your dad always got a better price for his quahogs because he always caught a lot. His stuff was perfect, and his bags were clean, no rocks." Russell's looking over my pile. "And if you're anything like your dad, which you seem to be, I want you selling to me every day."

I can't believe it. Russell's giving me a better price because of my dad. I must be in shock, because I can't believe what comes out of my mouth next.

"You gotta give *him* that price too," I say, pointing at Cliff.

"Aw, come on, Jake. I'm not giving some Long Islander three cents more." Russell is throwing his arms up in the air.

"Take it or leave it. That guy is my friend."

Russell rolls his eyes. "Aaaarrrhh. I must be crazy. All right, make it quick. I want to close up and get the hell out of here."

Russell deals with Cliff's load first, because I think he wants him out of here before any other locals come in and he has to explain why he's giving some Long Islander thirteen cents apiece.

Cliff stuffs a huge wad of money into his pocket and pulls me over to his truck. He reaches into the passenger seat and pulls out a paper bag with something heavy inside and hands it to me.

"Here is a little keepsake I dug up. I want you to have it so that you remember this day, because it was the best day of fishing anyone could ever have, and I'm honored to have been able to share it with *you*, Jake." He sticks out his hand and I shake it.

"Thanks. And thanks for saving my life out there." It's all I can manage to get out as he drives off, spitting white shells from his back tires. I watch the garvey bouncing on the trailer, moving north on Water Street, and just like that, he's gone. I open the bag and inside is a salty, barnacle-encrusted silver hood ornament from an old car. It's in the shape of a woman leaning forward, with two wings stretched back in aerodynamic flight. It's beautiful.

I stick it back in the bag and make my way back up to Russell's garage.

"That's too much to count at nine o'clock at night. Them five hundred bags, got a full count in each bag?"

"Yes, sir. Tommy counted them all day, and sometimes I made him count twice. Gene always made me count 'em twice."

"That's good enough for me, then." He starts peeling off bills and hands me a pile of cash.

"Twenty-six hundred and forty dollars. Should be all there. I counted it twice."

"That's good enough for me." I smile.

"Nice work today, Jake. You gonna get your own boat or keep using Gene's?"

"No, Gene will be back soon." I say this, but I don't really know. I promise myself I'll go visit him tomorrow.

"Well, if you do decide to get a boat, I'm sure we can work out a deal if you sell here."

"Thanks." I head back to my boat, where Tommy is asleep at the console.

I hand him two hundred bucks when I get down to the boat, but he won't take it.

"Get the hell outta here with that," Tommy says, pushing the money back at me. "Consider it my donation to the cause."

"Can you walk home or should I carry you?" I ask.

"You should carry me. I've never worked like that in my life."

"Hey . . . I don't know how to say this, but . . . thank you. You're the best."

"Don't ever forget that."

"I'll write it out and pin it to the wall at the diner."

"Hey," Tommy says, suddenly smiling. "I've got a date with Janna for the cabaret. That makes it all worthwhile."

"Better go get your beauty sleep, then." I'm laughing.

"Good deal," Tommy says as he walks slowly up the ramp to Water Street, rounding the corner.

I unlash the boat and drift back out into the Warren River and ride back to Gene's dock at full throttle. I'm stinking, sweaty, and I think for a minute that I'm rich. Then I catch myself, and I remember that I'm just one step closer to the ten thousand dollars.

My legs just barely push the pedals on my bike as I twist my way through the narrow streets, aiming toward home.

I can see my mom and Robin through the window, working in one of the booths. They have two pieces of white plywood hinged together at the top, and it's sitting on the table in front of them. They're each painting a side and smiling as they work. The sign says CABARET TONIGHT and some other stuff that I can't read from where I'm standing.

I want to run in there and throw the money down on the table and watch their faces when I tell them what I did. I want them to hug me and cry for joy and make me some dinner and send me to bed for three days straight. I want to feel like I've crossed the finish line somehow. But something is stopping me.

I still have one more thing to do.

25

THE ITALIAN–
AMERICAN CLUB
Tuesday night, August 24

Less than ten minutes later, I am running back down Water Street with almost six thousand dollars in my pocket. I'm hurting for the first two hundred yards, but then it feels good to stretch my legs and run. Each stride takes me closer to finishing this nightmare.

I slow down as I turn onto Kelly Street. There it is. The puke-colored cement building. It looks spookier at night, with neon beer signs in the windows and a single bare bulb above the door. *I hope he's there.* A brand-new black Cadillac is parked sideways in front of the doorway, taking up three spots, including the only handicapped parking spot. The Italian-American Club sign is reflected clearly on the polished hood of the car.

I'm terrified as I cautiously open the door. The smoke

hits me right away. It's the kind of smoke that smells like cigars that have been dipped in licorice booze.

"This is a private club. Members only." A fat guy with a close-cropped beard and slicked-back hair holds the door and blocks my way. He's looking up at me like I'm trick-or-treating on Christmas Eve.

"What's he want, Frank?" A larger man steps in. He's resting his fat fingers on a pool cue. I recognize him immediately as the guy named Cazzo, who comes to the Riptide.

"I want to see Mr. Vito."

"Listen kid, you can't just come in here and demand to see Mr. Vito. This ain't the Department of Motor Vehicles. You gotta have an appointment." Spittle from Frank's lips flies at my shirt.

I reach into my pocket and pull out the wad of bills and hold it up in the light. "I have some business to settle with him."

"Ooooh!" Cazzo laughs and slaps Frank on the back. "Looks like the kid's got an appointment after all. Step right in, kid." Cazzo pushes Frank out of the way.

I step inside and look around. The place looks like someone's remodeled basement, only bigger. It has cheap carpeting, with lots of cigarette burns and fake-wood paneling covered with posters showing girls in bikinis, holding bottles of beer. There's a pool table that's dimly lit and dark figures playing cards at two tables near the back.

"What's your name? I'll see if Vito wants to see you."

"Jake Cole."

"Okay, wait here." Frank heads off toward a small door. It has a black-and-gold sign that says OFFICE.

I watch Cazzo resume his pool game while I wait. The guy he's playing with leans over the cue ball to line up his shot. It's foggy with smoke swirling beneath the table's lights. I can barely see him. He looks familiar to me, his shape and his shoulders. I watch him miss his shot and throw his pool stick angrily onto a worn-out red leather couch. It bounces off and hits him in the shin. He looks around the room to see if anyone saw his errant shot, and he makes eye contact with me.

That's when I recognize him. *It's Paul. The guy whose rake I saved at the beach.* I can tell he recognizes me too, because his expression changes for an instant before he looks away and heads over to the bar. I wonder if he's here on business too.

Frank is leaning his head into the office doorway, and I can hear him talking to someone. It must be Mr. Vito.

"Yeah, the kid says his name is Jake Gold."

"Jake Cole!" I yell across the room.

"Yeah, right. Jake Cole," Frank repeats.

A second later this huge guy wearing a tan sport jacket, which I could easily use as a tent, comes through the door and waves me over. I hesitate for a second and look over to the bar, where Paul is ordering a beer and watching me carefully. Then I take the fifteen steps toward the office door and enter.

"I gotta go home. The wife expected me an hour ago," Frank says and heads over toward the coatrack. The huge guy just stands inside the door, jiggling a gold watch around his meaty wrist.

The office is a small room, with the same wood paneling on the walls and a cheap red carpet on the floor. Against one of the walls are silver racks overflowing with pots and pans and dry goods. There is a large black-lacquered desk with several ledgers and some silver-framed photos showing smiling faces of people on vacation somewhere tropical. Behind the desk is Vito.

He's wearing an oversize Patriots football jersey, and he's rolling the tip of his cigar into a crystal ashtray the size of a dinner plate. He takes off his glasses and rubs the bridge of his nose while squinting from fatigue.

"You John Cole's kid?" he asks without looking up.

"Yes."

"Sit down." He gestures with his cigar to the padded leather chair in front of his desk.

"I'd rather stand," I say, even though I am about to fall down.

Vito slips his glasses back onto his nose and looks me over. "Yeah, you're looking kinda grimy. You better stand."

"I just came from work," I say defensively.

"What are ya cleaning, cesspools?" the big guy says from behind me. Mr. Vito gestures with his index finger for the big guy to stop, and I look over my shoulder to see him cross his huge hands in front of himself like he's waiting at a funeral.

"So what can I do for you, John Cole's kid?" Vito leans back in his chair, and I can hear the leather shift with his weight.

"The Riptide . . . I have money for you." I pull the cash from my pocket and place it on the desk in front of him. The wad of bills splays open like a gutted fish, and Vito rests his elbows on the desk, looking it over but not touching it. He flips open one of the ledgers and runs a finger down a list.

"Cole, John." His finger taps the name. "Ten grand." He looks at me over the rims of his glasses. "It's all here?"

"No, not all of it."

He begins to move the bills with the tip of a pen like he's afraid to leave his fingerprints on them. "How much am I looking at here? What, six grand?"

"Fifty-seven hundred and fourteen dollars."

"You're walking around with fifty-seven hundred dollars in your pocket at what—fifteen, sixteen years old?"

"Fourteen."

"Fourteen?" He looks over at the guy by the door. "Hedge, you hear that—Christ, he's gonna be bigger than you someday."

"Doubt that," Hedge says, patting his belly.

"Where'd you get all this?" Vito looks at me.

"Does it matter?" I'm starting to feel that buzzing feeling spread through my body.

Vito looks at Hedge and puts his palms up. "Would you believe the set of coconuts on this kid?" Vito points his finger at me. "Now, you listen to me, you little snot. I've been very generous. Your mom hasn't made a payment in well over six months. You're lucky to still have that diner."

The buzzing is in my head now, so loud I can hardly hear him.

"And another thing, if I was a bank I would have repossessed that place months ago. Your dad used to make all his payments on time. What's the problem? Your mom drinking away all the profits?" He looks to Hedge and they both chuckle.

"My mom doesn't drink," I say sharply.

246

"Well, maybe she should. Probably get herself a new man."

I explode. Flying through the air, both hands outstretched, my fingers like talons going for his throat. I feel someone grab the back of my pants, and I stop mid-air and come crashing down on the edge of the desk. *Bang!* I drop to the floor, and I can feel my right eye swelling shut and the warm, wet sensation of blood leaking from my forehead.

"Hedge . . . why'd you do that? He's just a kid."

"I didn't do nuthin'. I just grabbed his belt when he lunged at you." Hedge lifts me up into a seated position on the floor to inspect the damage to my face.

"Clean him up and get some goddamned ice on that eye." Vito comes from around the desk and yells out into the bar. "Paul, get a bag of ice in here, quick."

My eye has totally shut now, and I can feel the swelling clear down to my cheek.

Paul comes running in with a bag of ice and stops short when he sees me on the floor. "What the—"

"Ice, ice." Hedge is waving his hand impatiently. Paul hands him the bag of ice and backs away toward the door.

"It was an accident. The kid fell over the chair," Vito says to him. Paul nods and leaves the office, and even through my one eye, I notice a glimmer of doubt on his face.

Hedge grabs my hand, sticks the ice in it, and then presses my palm against my eye. "Twenty minutes on, ten minutes off. Got it?"

I nod as cold waves immediately start to numb my face and hand. Vito moves to the chair in front of his desk and leans in close to me.

"That wasn't nice, kid." He steals a glance at the open door and talks to me in a harsh whisper, putting his finger inches from my nose. "I don't give a crap who your father was. You and your mom owe me forty-three hundred dollars by the thirty-first, or I'm taking that diner, understand?"

I nod silently.

"Good, I'm glad we've got that straight." Vito slaps me gently on the cheek, and I want to bite his fingers off. "Hell, at least I can turn it into something that'll make a profit." He gets up and grabs his jacket off the wall and heads out the door.

Hedge lifts me up to a standing position as easily as if I were made of straw. My knees give out and he catches me.

"Steady there, tiger," Hedge says.

Vito yells over his shoulder. "Paul, give Hedge a hand with the kid."

Paul comes in and throws one of my arms over

his shoulder, takes me from Hedge, and guides me to the door.

"You're a little wobbly, that's all. You'll be all right." He looks at my eye. "That'll go down tomorrow. I've had a hundred of those."

When he gets me to the door, I drop the ice and break into a run. I'm dazed and wobbling. I must look like I'm drunk.

I stop beneath a streetlamp in front of the liquor store and open my eyelid, exposing my eye to the light. The brightness burns, so I guess I'm not blind in that eye. My other eye is tearing, and it takes me a second to get my bearings. I start to jog down Water Street toward home.

My entire body is shaking as I move down the street, and in my head I'm playing out a hundred different scenarios that all end with me punching Vito so hard in the face that my hand comes out the other side like the way it happens in a cartoon. Each time I imagine it, the vision becomes goofier. By the time I get to the Riptide, I'm imagining I have these giant quahogs for hands and I'm batting his head back and forth like one of those blow-up punching dolls that keeps wobbling upright no matter how hard you hit it.

I'm laughing to myself as I open the screen door to the kitchen and step inside. Robin and my mom are there. My mom has her car keys in her hand. She drops them to the floor, runs over, and pulls me in so tight I can hardly breathe.

"Oh, thank God."

"It's okay, Mom." My voice is muffled in her hair.

She pulls away and twists my face into the light. "What happened to you? We were worried sick. Dave Becker came by to check on you hours ago. He said you started in from the beach at the same time he did. "

"I'll get some ice," Robin says, grabbing a dishtowel from the counter as my mom leads me into the restaurant like a Seeing Eye dog.

"How did this happen? Did you get into a fight?"

"No, nothing like that."

Robin comes back and hands me the dishtowel filled with ice. "Twenty minutes on . . ."

"And ten minutes off, I know," I say, taking the ice and holding it to my face.

Outside, a cop car pulls up to the front and Robin unlocks the door. The cop, who I recognize as Sergeant Justy, gets out of his car and pokes his head inside. "So you found him? He's okay?"

I hide my face behind the dishtowel and give him the thumbs-up sign.

"He's okay." My mother waves him off. "Thanks, Ralph."

Robin and my mom are all smiles at Sergeant Justy as he gets back into his car and pulls away.

Then they both turn on me.

"So now we want some answers, buster," Robin says.

"Tell us what's going on, Jake." My mom has her hand on my shoulder, and her eyes are pleading.

So I tell them how I worked the beach in Gene's boat and how Tommy was there and how we did really good and made almost twenty-seven hundred dollars.

"And then you went to the Italian-American Club, didn't you?" My mom's hand goes up in front of her mouth.

"I thought I could convince Vito to give us some more time."

"*He did this to you?* I'm going to kill that son of a . . ."

"No, Mom, it's not like that. He didn't do anything. It was an accident. I was such an Unco, I fell over his chair and smacked my head on his desk." I'm pleading with her to calm down.

She grabs my chin between her thumb and forefinger and turns my head to face her. "You swear to me those guys didn't touch a hair on your head. You swear to me, Jake Cole."

"I swear, Mom. I fell."

"You pull a stunt like that again, and I'll bust the other

eye," Robin says, heading back to the front door and turning the lock.

My mom pulls me into her arms, and I rest my head on her shoulder. "It's okay now. It's over, Jake." She starts rocking me slowly, and I just want to sleep right here. I feel myself drifting off, and the next thing I know, Robin and my mom are helping me up the stairs.

I climb into the tiny bed and I'm gone.

26

CENTER STAGE

Wednesday afternoon, August 25

I force my good eye open and stare at my alarm clock through the crust and film of a hard night's sleep.

3:45.

I am not sure if it is a.m. or p.m., but the sun shining through my window nudges me out of my haze. I feel like I could sleep through the night, but I know my mom, Darcy, and Robin have been working hard getting ready for the cabaret, and I should probably get downstairs and help out. The problem is, I feel like I've been run over by a tractor trailer. As I swing my legs over the side of the bed, my feet drop to the floor like anchors. My hands are clenched together as if they are still holding the rake, and I'm afraid to look at them. Searing-hot pain shoots up each arm as I work my fingers open. There are smudges of blood on the sheets. I'm not sure if it's from my blistered hands or the cut above my eye.

I'm a mess.

After taking inventory of the damage to my body, I take a hot shower. The water in the bottom of the tub is a mixture of mud, salt, sweat, and blood. I watch in a trance as it swirls down the drain. I dress and head downstairs.

Mom, Darcy, and Robin are running around, setting up everything. They have Christmas lights strung from the ceiling. The tables and booths have white cloths over them with candles stuck into old mayonnaise jars filled with sand.

"Afternoon, sleepyhead." Darcy zips past me, shaking some paper streamers in front of my face. "Wow, you look . . . you don't look so good."

"The last twenty-four hours have been a little rough." A humongous understatement, but I don't want to be a bummer right now because they all look really excited about this cabaret thing.

"How are you doing?" My mom comes rushing over and touches my face tenderly.

"I'm okay."

"So what do you think, Jake?" she asks, surveying the room.

"It looks nice. Festive. What can I do to help?"

"Well," she says, clapping her hands together, "I need you to run over to Tom Brennan's and pick up the lobsters. He donated fifty lobsters for tonight; isn't that great? Take the wheelbarrow. And when you get back, I need you to help build the stage for Robin."

"Stage?" I look over at the pile of wood in the corner.

"Of course. She's gotta have a stage. This is her big debut." My mom smiles at Robin as if Robin were her daughter. "Look, I even had the jukebox fixed, and Angelo from across the street lent us his sound system."

I must have a depressed look on my face because my mom pulls me over to one of the stools, and as I sit, she takes hold of my shoulders and looks me right in the eyes.

"Jake, I know this is all a little over-the-top, and it's probably a silly idea, and maybe I'm crazy for thinking we are going to raise enough money tonight to keep this place, but at least we can go out with a bang, right? What I am trying to say is, let's just have fun tonight. It's a party." She pulls me into a hug, and I can feel her tears on my cheek. "Oh, Jake, I know how hard you worked to save this place, and I know how much it means to you, how much your dad means to you. He would be so proud of you right now." She pulls back and runs her fingers through my hair. "I am so proud of you. You're the best son a mom could ever have."

I don't want to get all mushy with my mom, especially with Darcy there, so I get up to leave. "I'll go get those lobsters now, but I don't know how to build a stage."

"I don't need a stage. I'll probably sing only a couple of songs," Robin says.

"You are going to have a stage, Robin, and I don't want to hear another word about it," Mom says, wagging her finger like a conductor. Then she turns to me. "And somebody will help you, Jake, I am sure of it."

I head out the back door, and I can hear Darcy running after me. I slow down, and she catches up at the side of the house.

"Jake Cole!" she yells out like the principal at our middle school.

"Darcy Green!" I say back to her in a similar tone, but I don't look up as I empty the rainwater out of the wheelbarrow.

"Tommy said you were amazing out there yesterday."

"He did?" I glance back, and she's got her hands stuffed into her pockets.

"Yeah. He came by earlier looking for you, but I told him you were sleeping, which you were, and he told me to tell you that next time, *he* gets to be the captain."

"He said that?" I laugh.

"So much for the whole *I gotta do this alone* thing, huh?" she says, imitating me from yesterday. "Oh, and he was also blabbering on about this Janna girl that was out there, but he must have been seeing things, right? You told me yourself there weren't going to be any girls out there."

"Aw, come on, Darce," I plead for forgiveness.

"I'm just messing with you." She laughs. "I actually just wanted to come out and tell you that I'm proud of you too. I heard things didn't go so well at the Italian Club." She's pointing her finger to her eye and staring at mine.

"Yeah, not so good."

"Bastards." Darcy kicks some shells on the ground. "How much do you still need?"

"Too much," I say, walking away from her with the wheelbarrow. As I'm walking, I know it's wrong, but I can't face her. I feel shattered.

"Jake?"

"I gotta go."

Walking over to Tom Brennan's with the wheelbarrow, I'm totally depressed. There is a hole in my stomach that all the fried-egg sandwiches in the world could never fill.

• • •

Getting back to the Riptide with more than a hundred and twenty pounds of lobsters in a wheelbarrow is not easy. I have to stop every fifty feet or so to pick up the escapees. I push the wheelbarrow over the curb in front of Muldoon's, losing control, and dump half of them onto the sidewalk. A couple guys from inside come out to help.

"Where you going with all these beauties, Jake?"

"The Riptide's having a cabaret tonight. It's twenty bucks a head. We're having lobsters, chowder, stuffies, and live music. You should tell your friends inside." They look a bit doubtful, so I add, "And all the beer and wine you can drink."

"I thought you guys didn't have a liquor license."

"Who's going to complain, you?" I press.

"Not me." He laughs. "You gonna complain, Sam?"

"Definitely not," Sam says, "I'll be wearing my drinking shoes!" Sam looks down at my hands. "Jesus, those mitts of yours look like raw hamburger. I heard you worked the beach yesterday. I didn't see you out there."

"That would be like finding a needle in a haystack," I say.

"How'd you make out?" he asks.

"I did fine, I guess." I don't really want to say. Gene always says don't ever talk about what you caught, because if it was even one more quahog than they caught, they'll be on you like flies on dog crap the rest of the week. So I don't say anything more than that.

"Fine? Bainsey said you hauled in forty-eight bags, almost sunk Gene's boat. That's what Bainsey said. Is it true?"

"Something like that. Listen, thanks for your help with the lobsters. I gotta get 'em back to the Riptide before they die in this heat. Don't forget to tell your friends about the cabaret tonight."

As I wheel away, I can still hear them talking.

"There's no way that kid caught forty-eight bags. I only got thirty-eight myself, and I was out there until dusk."

"Quit your bellyaching and go buy me another drink, 'cause I only got thirty-five bags, you peckerhead."

I just continue wheeling those lobsters down the street, but I can't help smiling the rest of the way.

With the lobsters in the kitchen and my mom working away on the chowder and stuffed quahogs, I head out front to tackle building a stage. I swear to God, I am going to drop dead by the time the cabaret starts. Every muscle in my body aches.

Next to the jukebox I see five long two-by-fours leaning up against the wall and two sheets of plywood on the floor. Honestly, I don't know where to begin. I've never built anything out of wood in my life, and now I have an hour to build a stage for Robin's singing-career debut.

I know there are some nails and a saw and hammer in the basement, but as I turn to get them, I freeze. Standing in the doorway is Gene. He looks weak, but he's smiling and holding his toolbox with his good arm.

"I heard we got us a stage to build," Gene says.

"Gene, you're home!" I run over to him and want to give him a bear hug, but I know he's weak, so I give him a half hug and a pat on the back. I want to tell him all about the beach and how I caught forty-eight bags and almost sank his boat but didn't, and that I was sorry I took his boat without asking, and how I got back too late to get a good price, and how crazy it was out there on the water, but I can't actually say anything. I have a fist-size lump in my throat, and I just want to bury my face in his flannel shirt and cry, because I'm so glad he's here right now.

"You look like you've been through the wringer. What happened to your eye?"

"Oh, that? I just fell. It was stupid, really."

Gene takes both my hands in his and turns them over for inspection. He winces. "Did you slay 'em out there? I heard you slayed 'em."

Gene and I spend the next hour putting together the makeshift stage. I do most of the sawing and hammering, while Gene is the brains of the operation. The whole time we talk about the beach as he lobs questions at me one after another.

"Were the quahogs layered up on each other?" Gene asks, handing me the pencil.

"Yeah, just like you said. It was mud but it felt like hard bottom, they were so thick."

"And what about off of the seventeenth hole?"

"Yeah, as soon as the wind picked up, I went over there, right up by Rumstick Rock, just like you said. It was perfect."

"I knew it." Gene has a faraway look in his eyes.

"You should have been there, Gene. You would've caught a hundred bags."

"Well, you were in my boat, using my rake, so it was just like I was there. And I don't know about a hundred bags. That old Hawkline would've sunk for sure," Gene says. I hammer in the last nail.

"It better not fall apart when Robin hits her high note." Darcy gracefully leaps onto our newly built stage. I am currently eye level with her bare knees as she pretends to be doing a guitar solo, and Gene and I whistle as she bounces around like a rock star.

I grab a Coke and head toward one of the stools by the counter. I choose the one that's got silver tape across the top holding the cushion in place, figuring if I sit on this one, the rest of them don't look so bad. My mom swishes from table to table, lighting candles and humming to the song on the jukebox. Trax and Robin are rolling silverware into paper napkins. Darcy is helping Gene carry his toolbox.

I wish it could stay like this forever.

27
LETTING GO
Wednesday evening, August 25

There's no way we're going to get forty-three hundred dollars to Vito by the end of the month. I've done the math in my head a bunch of times. It's over, and I'm trying to accept it, but the feeling is like someone has just drained all the fluid from my body, and I'm moving through life in a dry, brittle shell. The slightest breeze is going to carry me off in a million pieces, like dust in the desert.

Here I come, Arizona. Dad, I hope you can find me there.

I pedal slowly down New Meadow Road toward Gene's house. I can't see much out of my right eye, and I don't want to crash my bike. I don't think my body can take any more punishment.

Ten minutes later I drop my bike onto his shell driveway and start jogging down to the dock.

Good. They're still there.

I climb aboard the Hawkline and carefully remove my dad's glasses from the bungee cord holding them to the console. The lenses have tiny circles of salt on them, and I lick them clean and wipe them off on my shirt. The salt tastes good on my tongue. I'm sure I have salt water in my veins now too.

"I'm sorry, Dad. I wanted to save the Riptide, but I couldn't." I'm sitting on the gunwale, staring at the glasses in my hand. "I know that if you were here, you wouldn't let this happen, but you're not."

I miss you, Dad. I miss you so much.

I put the glasses on and everything goes blurry. I slump down onto the deck so I don't fall overboard, and I let the tears come.

It feels good to cry until there's nothing left. I'm dried out like that plant in the window my mom keeps forgetting to water. Empty.

And then something happens. It feels like the tide is coming into my body and filling me up. I can feel the strength returning to my arms and legs, and that empty feeling is starting to leave me. I stay there like that, without moving for a while.

Suddenly, I feel a peck on my leg. I take the glasses off and see that it's Jessy. She's staring at me as if she wants to say something.

"Hey, girl."

Jessy cranes her head around, pecks at the knots of fishing line wrapped around her leg, and then stares at me expectantly.

A final test.

I reach into my pocket for my knife. I open the blade and place it on the deck. "It's okay, girl. I'm just gonna cut that fishing line off your leg. It's all right." I'm inches away, closer to her than I've ever been, and Jessy hasn't moved at all. I touch the feathers behind her head, and she jumps a little bit, but stays within reach. On the next try, I start behind her head, then move my right hand farther down her wing feathers and gently cradle her under my arm. She seems calmer as I stroke her head with my hand. I shift her body to expose her chafed leg, which is red and raw. The clear fishing line is thick and knotted but loose enough to slip the knife blade beneath. She kicks her other leg as if she's paddling while I work the knife blade. The fishing line is cut through, and I remove the monofilament cuff from her leg. She's ready to fly. I leg go, and she catches herself in the breeze, just off the starboard side of the boat, hovering there for a few

265

seconds. With a shrill caw, Jessy lifts to the sky, and now, we are both free.

I don't have to swim that rock anymore.

When I finally get up to leave, I feel okay. Not great, but okay. I pick up my dad's glasses and look at them. "Dad, we're having a cabaret at the Riptide tonight. I don't want you to miss it." I fold the frames carefully and put them in my shirt pocket, grab my bike, and head home.

When I arrive at the Riptide, I see Gene sleeping in an old beach chair by the seawall. He awakens when I roll up.

"Where have you been?" He gets up slowly, leaning heavily on his good arm. His eyes are red against the driftwood-colored paleness of his skin.

"I had to get something from the boat. What are you doing out here? Why aren't you inside? Are you okay?" I rush over and help him get up.

"Don't worry about me. I was just taking a little cat-nap before the big party. They still got me on a bunch of pills, and I get tired real quick." Gene looks out over the water. "You sure have a nice view of the river."

He turns back to me, and that's when he notices my dad's glasses sticking out of my shirt pocket. "He was out there with you, at the beach?" Gene smiles.

"I guess he was looking after me."

"He's looking after all of us, Jake," Gene says with a quick glance skyward.

"Should we go in?" I ask.

"You lead the way." Gene smiles.

I head inside with Gene, and I can't believe how many people are here. I have never seen it so full, not even the day after the hurricane. Everyone is here: Dave Becker, Bainsey, C. J., Brendan Tooley, Jay Miller, even Russell. I see Tommy's dad behind the counter, pouring drinks into plastic cups, and Billy Mac is sitting on a stool near the door, collecting the money as people walk in. A few of the guys come over to talk to Gene and ask him how he's doing, and I go and find my mom sitting at a table near the jukebox.

"What can I do, Mom?"

"I told you, Jakey, you've done enough. Everything else is taken care of. Trax is back there in the kitchen dealing with the food; Mr. Clancy is working the bar; Darcy and Robin can handle the rest. You just relax. Dance, eat, and for God's sake, have fun!" she orders jokingly, then smiles at Gene, who is making his way over to the table.

"This is quite a spread, Maggie." My mom pulls back a chair for Gene and places a cushion behind his upper back as he gingerly sits down next to her.

"Hey, Jake, nice shiner." Tommy comes over, balancing

a large Coke and a plate full of stuffed quahogs. "Oh, hey, Mrs. C. These stuffies are wicked good." Tommy pulls me aside and whispers in my ear. "Don't look now, Jake, but check it out. Twelve o'clock."

I follow Tommy's eyes across the room. In booth number three is Janna Miller. She is sitting with her dad, eating lobster and laughing with Dave Becker and some other quahogger. She is completely relaxed and smiling, with those brilliant white teeth that glow from her tanned face.

"I am totally going to ask her to dance," Tommy says.

"Since when do you dance?"

"Since tonight." Tommy elbows me, and we go find some empty folding chairs near the back, where we both have a good view of Janna. Suddenly my view is blocked, and I look up, and Darcy is holding a lobster dinner in front of me.

"Where have you been, Stretch?" she asks, handing me the lobster. "This is the last one, but I saved it for you."

"Thanks, Darce, that was nice." I smile.

"How's your eye? Do you want me to get you some ice?"

"I'll take some ice," Tommy says, holding up his plastic cup. "For my Coke."

Darcy glares at him. "Oh, I'm sorry, Tommy. I didn't know your legs were broken. The bar is right over there." Darcy points to the counter, where Tommy's dad smiles back at us and waves. Tommy looks at me with a wide-eyed smirk as Darcy pulls another chair over next to mine and sits down so that our legs are just brushing up against each other. My ears get hot. The three of us sit in the back and look out over the scene while we eat.

"This was a good idea, Darce." I look over at her, and her eyes meet mine.

"Thanks, Jake."

My stomach does a little flip because she never calls me Jake, unless she's really mad about something. I have to look away, so I focus on my dinner, trying not to fling lobster juice on her clothes.

"Hey, where's Robin? This is her big night, and I don't see her anywhere." Darcy stands up and scans the room.

"I saw her heading out back," Tommy says with a mouth full of quahog stuffing. "She was looking a little green."

"Let me go get her. I have to thank her anyway," I say as Darcy sits down and grabs a stuffed quahog off of Tommy's plate.

"Yeah, go ahead. Help yourself," Tommy says to her mockingly.

"I'll be right back." I head through the double doors and into the kitchen.

Trax is pouring hot water into the double sink, and

the steam is circling his head like a halo. He sees me and nods toward the back door. I step outside and see Robin sitting by the seawall. She's wearing a green silk dress, and her hair is down, and she's sitting on her hands and rocking back and forth. I hesitate for a second, thinking she might want to be alone, but then I head over.

"Anyone sitting here?" I sit down on the wall next to her.

"I can't do it," Robin says, staring into the water. "I thought I could, but I'm just shaking all over."

"You mean singing? Darcy says you're singing all the time." I start throwing small shells into the water.

"Yeah, that's after the diner is closed and everyone's gone home and it's just me and Darcy and your mom." Robin turns to face me. "Did you see all those people in there?"

"Yeah, but you know all those people. They're going to think you're great even if you sing like a frog."

"Jake, I know this means a lot to your mom . . . and you. . . . I feel terrible. She put so much into this, and you and Gene built that stage and I'm so ashamed. I can't . . . I just can't." Robin gets up to leave.

"Robin, wait."

"I'm sorry, Jake."

"Come on, just listen to me." Robin stops and looks

at me. I've got my hands on my hips, and I'm looking down and kicking the dirt, trying to think.

"I'm listening."

"Okay, well, look." I turn my palms up. "I mean, just yesterday I worked the beach, right?"

"Yeah?" Robin draws it out, slowly trying to figure out what I'm getting at.

"Well, I never actually did that before. Gene let me pull the rake on his lunch breaks and stuff, and that's how I practiced, but I never actually did it on my own." I'm on a roll now, and I just keep talking because I can see Robin starting to relax. "I was so scared I was going to mess up, or do something stupid, or sink Gene's boat, and there were about four thousand quahoggers out there, and I almost didn't go."

"But you did."

"Yeah, I did. And it was still scary at first because I didn't really know what I was doing. There were so many boats and guys yelling, and it was crazy. But I just put my head down and did what I knew how to do, and after a little while I wasn't scared anymore. I mean it was hard, but it wasn't scary. It was actually fun."

"Would you do it again?

"In a second."

Robin is looking up at me, and her eyes begin to

smile. "Jake, you're something else, you know that?" She points her finger at me and sneers. "All right, I'll do it. But if they laugh me at me in there because I freeze up or my voice squeaks . . ."

"Or the stage breaks?" I snicker.

"Or if the stage breaks. I am going to have your head on a platter. You got me, mister?"

"Ten-four."

Robin puts her hands over her mouth and lets out an anguished sigh and shakes her head, as if not believing what she is about to do. I watch her as she walks back through the door of the Riptide.

I start to follow when Captain—*George Hassard*—steps out of the shadows.

"That was quite a speech."

I stare in shock.

"What? You look like you've seen a ghost or something, kid."

"You're out." I'm looking over my shoulder for the cops, thinking that George probably broke out of jail somehow.

"Out?" He laughs. "I was never in."

"But I saw you . . . the other night . . . when we went striper fishing."

"*Pffft!*" George throws his hand up. "That prick Delvecchio didn't have anything on me. I was home watching the Red Sox before they finished the paperwork."

"I thought it was because of that night they caught us out dredging."

"But they didn't catch us, did they?" He's looking at me out of the corner of his eye. "You didn't let 'em board the boat. Smartest thing you could have done."

"So are you still doing it?"

"What? Dredging?" George smirks. "Nah, the damn beach opening screwed the pooch on that one. The price is so low it's not even worth my time. I'm trapping tautog now. These fish are so stupid, I don't have to use any bait. They just swim right into the traps for me. I got forty-six Chinese restaurants that'll buy every fish I catch. The goddamned DEM don't even know how to regulate it. It's a thing of beauty, Jake. Thing is, I need a deckhand."

"Gene's home, you know. I'll be working for him now."

"Come on, Jake, I could really use you out there."

"I got to go, George." I reach for the back door and add, "Gene's waiting for me." I shut the door behind me and don't look back.

I head back through the party, breathing a sigh of relief, when suddenly I get slapped on the back.

"Jake, you killed them out there yesterday." Dave

Becker is smiling at me from ear to ear. "Russell told me you and your buddy came in with a huge haul. How are those hands?"

I raise both hands and break out into a smile as a bunch of the other guys gather around to inspect them.

"Ooooohhh! Welcome to the club!" Dave holds his hands up next to mine. He's got these huge calluses at each joint, and his palms look like truck tires.

They're all laughing now and sharing stories and showing off their battle wounds, and I feel like my dad is right here, standing next to me. I want to remember this forever.

I take his glasses from my shirt pocket and bring them over to the register. I carefully place them back on top, looking out at the scene, knowing, somehow, that he's seeing all this.

28

THE CABARET

Wednesday night, August 25

"Robin's going to sing now, Jake, come on." Darcy grabs my hand and pulls me back to our chairs.

Darcy watches intently as Robin makes her way onto the makeshift stage. I look over, and my mom is frantically turning off the jukebox and plugging in the microphone.

"This should be a hoot," Tommy says sarcastically, and Darcy shoots him a glare that almost knocks me over.

"Good evening, everybody." My mom is on the stage with her arm around Robin. My mom taps her hand on the microphone to get everyone's attention.

"All right, all right, settle down," my mom says into the mike, with a smile.

Robin looks like she wants to run.

"Thank you all for coming to the cabaret. And what's a cabaret without live music! We have a special treat tonight. The beautiful Robin McCaphrey is going to be making her singing debut right here at the Riptide! So I want you all to give her a warm welcome." The Riptide echoes with applause, and I can't believe it. I haven't seen my mom that talkative and sure of herself since before my dad disappeared. I think for a second that *she* might start singing.

Robin takes the microphone, and the whole place gets real quiet. She closes her eyes and begins to sing "Stormy Weather." She starts out real soft and you can hardly hear her. Then, opening her eyes slowly, she starts to sway slightly, and her voice gains strength.

I know the song because my mom used to play it all the time on the jukebox, when I was little. Robin can sing great; her voice sounds better than the record. Everyone is watching her like they're in a trance.

"She's amazing," I say, looking at Darcy.

"I bet your mom didn't realize how much talent she had working for her." Darcy smirks.

Robin comes to the end of the song, and the Riptide erupts into cheers and applause. She's grinning and staring down at the stage, too overwhelmed to look up. She sings another song that has the whole diner swaying right along with her.

My mom gets a bunch of people to leave their seats

and start pushing the tables off to the side, clearing out an area in front of the stage. Darcy, Tommy, and I get up to help her, although I think it's kind of rude to kick people out after only a couple of songs.

"What are we doing, Mom?" I ask as we carry a large table over toward the kitchen.

"What does it look like, Jake? We're making a dance floor!"

Robin takes the cue perfectly and starts belting out another song with a more upbeat tempo. The dance floor quickly fills right up. Everybody is dancing and singing along, and it seems that the Riptide is becoming a night-club earlier than expected.

I watch with awe as Tommy walks straight up to Jay Miller's table and asks Janna to dance. I feel for Tommy because Janna is way out of his league, and Jay Miller's probably going to throttle him for asking. I'm shaking my head and laughing as Janna takes his hand and Tommy leads her out to the dance floor. I can't believe it, and before I know what's happening, Darcy pulls me out there too.

"I can't dance." I stand, still looking at her.

"What? Everybody can dance."

"I can't." I head back over to our chairs to sit down. I feel bad, because I want to dance with Darcy, but I know I'll probably spaz out and break her foot or maybe my own.

"What's the deal?" Darcy plops down next to me.

"I'm totally uncoordinated. Seriously, someone will get hurt."

"Jake—you just went out and caught like a bazillion quahogs yesterday. You call that uncoordinated?"

"That was on the water."

"What?" Darcy looks at me, puzzled.

"The water. When I'm out on the water, everything works. Everything does what I tell it to do." I start flailing my arms and legs. "But on land I'm an Unco. I can't explain it."

Darcy grabs my hand and yanks me back over to the dance floor, also grabbing a half-filled water glass from an empty table on the way. She empties the glass onto the floor at my feet.

"There. Now you're on water. Let's dance."

And we dance.

And I'm not clumsy or Unco or spastic, and I don't break her foot. We just dance. I'm still not that good, and I don't know all the moves, but Darcy takes the lead and I let her, and we dance like that for three songs straight.

Tommy is dancing with Janna right next to us, and he keeps looking over, giving me the thumbs-up.

Then Robin sings another slow song, and I start to

head back to my chair. Before I get halfway there, Darcy drags me off to an empty booth and forces me to sit. She looks like an angel as her eyes sparkle.

Without taking her eyes off me, she removes her sweater and throws it into the booth. She is wearing a beautiful summer dress, with thin little straps that gracefully swoop over her shoulders and get lost in her hair.

There it is, out for everyone to see; her naked arm, in all of its beautiful, intricate, twisted scarring, like a big tattoo that reaches from her shoulder to her hand.

I rise up and put my hands on her shoulders. She's trembling, and little pools of water well up in the corners of her eyes.

"Are you sure?" I ask.

Darcy nods silently.

"And you want to go dance?" I ask.

"Uh-huh."

"Okay. But before we go out there, I want to tell you something. I just want to say . . . I mean . . . you're the coolest person I've ever met and I'm happy . . . I'm really glad that you are here with me, with us."

I take her hand and lead her back out to the dance floor. Darcy is looking down, afraid to see the reactions of everybody, but I'm taking it all in with my head up, as we walk together to the middle of the floor.

"It's all cool, Darce. They're all cool, trust me," I whisper in her ear.

Darcy throws both arms over my shoulders, resting her head on my chest. Then she tilts her head back to look at me, and I don't look anywhere else but in her eyes, and we dance slow, even though the music is fast, and everyone dances around us as if nothing has changed.

But I know everything's different now.

Robin takes a final bow to thundering applause and quickly steps down off the stage. My mom tackles her into a hug, and Robin leans over to me and says, "You're right, Jake. I was terrified at first, but once I got going, I loved it!"

Brendan Tooley takes Robin's place behind the microphone and starts belting out a slightly changed and out-of-tune version of a country song.

Mommas, don't let your babies
grow up to be clammers!

Everyone in the place chimes in:

DON'T LET 'EM DIG QUAHOGS
AND DRIVE THEM OLD TRUCKS,
LET 'EM BE DOCTORS AND LAWYERS
AND SUCH!

I am laughing so hard I don't realize that Darcy is still holding my hand. She notices me glancing down and quickly lets go and starts clapping and singing with everyone else. Brendan shouts out a few more rounds, and then throws his hands up in the air like he just won a singing contest. I'm sure he's drunk.

"All right, all right, thank you, Brendan, for that country classic." Jay Miller has the microphone now, and everyone gets real quiet because Jay doesn't ever talk too much.

"First off, how about a big hand for Maggie Cole, who put this shindig together?" My mom turns red as a tomato and waves Jay off as everyone turns to her, hooting and hollering.

"Before John Cole built this diner, he was the best quahogger on Narragansett Bay. You know that's a fact. And I don't know how many of you were at Barrington Beach yesterday . . ." Laughter ripples through the crowd. "His son, Jake, was out there yesterday, and he outcaught most of us."

Now it's my turn to get red in the face, and I want to hide behind the counter. Tommy slaps me on the back and I hear, "Atta boy, Jake!"

"So I propose a toast." Jay raises his plastic cup high into the air. "To the Coles!"

"To the *Coles!*" everyone shouts.

Then, just like that, a wave of silence washes over the diner. I'm wondering what's going on, and as I look over people's heads, I can see why.

Standing in the doorway is Paul, and next to him is Vito. It's obvious that most of the people in here know who he is, because they are all quiet and watching. My mom comes over and lays a protective hand on my shoulder.

Vito nods to a few people as he winds through the crowd and makes his way toward the stage.

"What is *he* doing here?" my mom says in a harsh whisper.

"I guess he paid his twenty bucks, I don't know," I respond, but I'm nervous too. I'm also wondering what Paul is doing here with him.

Vito steps up onto the stage and puts his hand out to Jay. "May I?" Jay reluctantly hands him the microphone and steps off. Paul looks around nervously as he waits by the door.

"Well, I certainly didn't mean to stop the party." Vito laughs to himself and holds out his hand. "I just want to say a few words." Vito squints at the door. "Paul, get up here." Paul drops his head and works his way toward the stage. A path clears in front of him, and I'm wondering what the heck is going on. Paul climbs up onstage and stands there like he just got detention. If the stage doesn't break now, it never will.

"I know a lot of you know me. Hell, I helped most of you buy your houses and boats and whatever, but I don't know if you know my son, Paul." Vito puts his arm around Paul, and the poor guy looks like he wants to puke. "Well, my boy was out there with you all yesterday, and he was having some trouble. It's not easy, what you guys do, and I appreciate that. But Paul here is not one to ask for help. Stubborn like his dad, I guess."

"Get to the point," Brendan Tooley barks.

Vito scans the audience until he finds Brendan and gives him a hard look. "Hey, Brendan," he says, smiling, "you want to keep that new boat of yours? Then shut your trap." Vito turns back to the crowd, pinching the bridge of his nose with his thumb and forefinger. "Where was I? . . . Jake Cole, come up here."

I feel a thousand eyes on me, and my mom holds me back, but I step forward anyway. I don't think the guy is going to do anything with all these witnesses, but even so, my palms are slick with sweat.

Vito reaches out his hand, and I take it and he pulls me up onto the stage. "This kid helped my son out yesterday. He wasn't asked to, he wasn't paid to . . . he just did it."

I look over at Paul, and he nods at me, but his eyes look away quickly.

"Now, stuff like that builds community," Vito says, resting one arm across the microphone stand. "And I'm all about community. Jimmy! Who helped you get that new engine for your boat?"

"You did." Jimmy Paterno grunts from the back of the diner.

"That's right. And who helped Gus Bellman rebuild when his shoe store burned down?"

"You," a few voices grumble.

"So you see, I'm all for community, just like Jake here." Vito reaches into his jacket pocket and pulls out a stack of folded papers and hands it to me.

"What's this?" I ask, taking the papers.

"Give that to your mom. She'll know what to do with them." Vito takes a look around the room. "Nice place. Come on, Paul, let's go." Vito tries putting the microphone back in the stand but quickly gives up and drops it on the floor, where it lands with a loud thump and a squeal of feedback. Everyone watches in a dumbfounded silence as they exit the door.

My mom, Robin, Darcy, and Tommy rush the stage.

"One heck of a way to serve an eviction notice!" My mom grabs the papers from my hand and quickly opens them.

The first page is a slightly torn sheet of green paper that reads: "Save the Riptide! Come to the Cabaret!" in big letters across the top. I recognize the handwriting immediately and stare at Tommy.

"What? I got a friend that works at the copy shop." Tommy shrugs.

"And you gave one to *Vito*?" I ask.

"No, I just put one on his car. Darcy had me make like three hundred copies. I wasn't gonna waste 'em."

My mom flips to the next page. It looks official, with lots of small writing and a few embossed stamps on the bottom.

"What's it say?" I plead. "Do we have to leave now?"

She is holding it close to her face as she reads, and I can see her hands begin to shake, and without warning she throws her arms around me, and then Darcy and Tommy and Robin squeeze us all together.

"What is it, Mom?"

"It's the deed, Jake." She's crying now. "It's the deed to the Riptide. We own it now, free and clear!"

We are not moving to Arizona.

29
THE FRESHMEN
Tuesday morning, September 7

I wake up at five thirty. I don't have to be at school until seven thirty, but I put on some old jeans and a T-shirt and head downstairs anyway. Since the cabaret, business at the Riptide has been great, and my mom has been really happy.

I see Gene sitting in the last booth by the window. He must have snuck in. He still looks pale, but he's much stronger and told me he'll be able to get back out in the boat before the end of the month. He has something wrapped in newspaper on the table in front of him.

"Morning, Jake." His eyes have that concerned look, and his eyelids are quivering like he's thinking hard about something.

"What are you doing here so early?"

"Whaddya think, Jake? This is a big day." Gene looks nervous, fiddling with the wrapping paper. "I wanted to wish you luck on your first day of high school, what else?"

I slide into the booth across from Gene, and he pushes the package in front of me. I open it up and see that it's a picture frame. Turning it over, I see a photograph of me, bullraking at Barrington Beach. There's Tommy, sitting on huge pile of quahogs, with a million boats in the background. Along the bottom is a newspaper clipping that reads, LOCAL QUAHOGGERS HIT IT BIG.

I lift it up to get a good look. Gene smiles, and tears begin to well up in his eyes.

"This is awesome! How'd you get this?" I ask.

"Johnny Bennato's got friends everywhere, even on the newspaper staff. They were out there taking pictures all day."

"This is definitely going up on that wall," I say, pointing to the pictures and memorabilia above the counter.

"You'll find a spot for it."

I pull the knife out of my pocket and place it on the table in front of him. Gene picks it up and turns it over in his hand, with a knowing smile.

"Where did you get this?" he says, studying the pearl inlays.

"It's my dad's. George gave it to me." I say this

287

reluctantly, still almost afraid to mention his brother. "You know I worked for him, while you were in the hospital."

"I know. Your mother told me. My brother and I used to be close, but now . . ." Gene's voice drifts off and he stares out the window.

He holds the knife out. "We all have one."

"A knife, like this?"

"Your father made this. He made one for all of us . . . me, George, and himself." Gene hesitates. "He made one for you too, you know."

"He did?"

"He wanted you to have it when you were old enough, when you were ready." Gene taps the glass on the picture frame. "I guess you're ready now, huh?"

"You have it?"

"It's here. It's been here all along, Jake." Gene points above the counter, where the striped bass is mounted. "It's inside that."

I rush over and grab a step stool and place it under the fish. My dad caught this fifty-pound striper the week before I was born and had it mounted as a trophy. I reach up and try to take it down but quickly realize that the wooden backing is screwed to the wall.

"Reach into his mouth," Gene calls over.

I carefully put my hand into the fish's open mouth,

past his teeth, pushing through cobwebs and into the hollow of his belly. And I feel it. Just like the one I've been carrying around in my pocket for weeks.

Thank you, Dad.

I look at the knife, and with my thumb I rub the dust off one side, revealing the initials.

J. M. C. Jake Michael Cole. *My name.*

"Wow. I don't know what to say. I owe you." I walk back over to the booth.

Gene gets all scrunched up in the face, and he's struggling to speak. "Owe me? Jake . . . what do you mean?" He pauses and then says, "You saved my life."

"No, I didn't. Your brother saved your life."

"No, Jake, I mean . . . you saved my life, this life." Gene starts gesturing around the room, the stools, the pictures on the walls, and then slaps both hands down on the table and rubs them across it as if it were made of the finest hardwood.

"I never even had a real life before this. I was going nowhere, digging every day, making money with nothing to spend it on but that old boat in my yard. Now you've given me something to love, something to care about. I mean, take a look at my brother—he doesn't have that. He's a pirate, chasing thrills. He doesn't care about anybody."

I'm not sure what he's saying, and I must have a

puzzled look on my face because he reaches across the table and grabs both my arms and leans in close to me.

"You did it, Jake. Don't you understand? You saved this place. You and your mom and the memory of your dad . . . that's my family. They were going to take that all away, and you saved it."

Gene pauses, and his head is moving from side to side like he's searching for something. "I guess what you always want in life is right in front of you, and you have to treasure it, and you have to love it enough to do whatever it is to keep it safe and protected. Isn't that the way it is?"

"I learned that from you a long time ago," I say, suddenly understanding him.

"Isn't that the way it is?" he repeats.

"That's the way it is."

Just then, there is a loud rapping sound on the window. We both look to see Darcy and Tommy standing at the door, backpacks in hand and all ready to go to school. We still have an hour before school starts. Tommy leans his head into the doorway.

"Come on, Jake, you're not ready. Even Darcy's already dressed." Darcy punches Tommy on the arm.

"I'll be ready in a minute. Come inside and wait."

Darcy walks in like a runway model, moving her hips from side to side, showing off her new jeans and a new shirt. It's not short-sleeved, but it isn't quite long-sleeved either.

"Hi, Tommy. Who's your friend?" Gene pretends not to recognize her.

Tommy gets down low and points to Darcy's butt. "New jeans, meet old Gene. Old Gene, this is New Jeans."

Gene starts laughing. "Tommy, I may be a little beat up, but I'm far from old."

I grab the knives and the photo and head up to my room to get changed. I get dressed quickly and loop my belt as I come down the stairs. Tommy's at the bottom step, and I have to move around him as I enter the diner.

"You didn't miss a step," he says.

"And you didn't conk your head," Darcy adds, and they are both staring at me.

"Yeah, I guess I didn't."

"So, maybe it's not gonna be Jake Unco this year?" Tommy smiles.

"Yeah, that'd be good. What about you?" I ask, looking at Tommy's sneakers, all glued together.

"Oh, I'll always be Trashman Tommy, but what they don't get is, I really don't care."

"If the shoe fits." Darcy gently kicks his sneakers.

"Come on, let's go." Tommy starts dragging us toward the door.

Gene gets up from the booth slowly, groaning as he stretches to stand.

"You guys go ahead. I'll catch up." I stand next to Gene as they head out the door.

"You have some great friends there," Gene says.

"Yeah, I do."

I lean in and give Gene a big hug, and he hugs me back and I feel like he's never going to let go.

"Take it slow, with your shoulder and all," I say, pulling away.

"Aye, aye." Gene slaps me on the back. "Now get the hell out of here. Go get a bushel of A's this year. I'll see you for breakfast tomorrow."

As I move up the street, I look back through the window to see Gene greeting my mom as she puts on her apron. She has a flower in her hair, and she's smiling at him as he walks over to the counter.

I catch up with Tommy and Darcy about a block away, and I slide my hand into hers. She takes it and holds on for two blocks as the three of us walk silently.

When we get there, Tommy stops abruptly at the bottom of the front steps of the high school. We're still early, with just a few kids waiting outside. Vinny Vile and Jim Allen are kicking the backpacks that are lined up against the wall as they head inside.

"Oh, crap," Tommy says. "Some things never change."

Darcy pulls Tommy and me in close, and the three of us are in a tight huddle.

"Let's do this together," Darcy says.

"That's cool with me." Tommy nods in agreement.

"It's the only way," I say as we start up the steps and walk through the open front door.

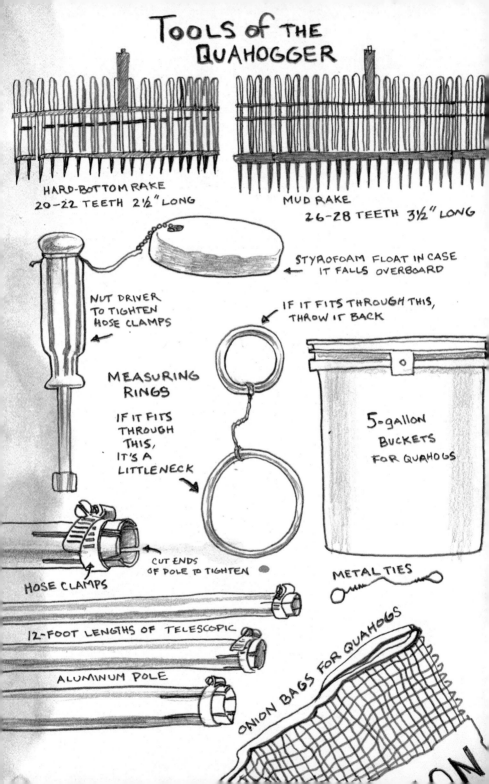

Tools of the Quahogger

HARD-BOTTOM RAKE
20–22 TEETH 2½" LONG

MUD RAKE
26–28 TEETH 3½" LONG

STYROFOAM FLOAT IN CASE IT FALLS OVERBOARD

NUT DRIVER TO TIGHTEN HOSE CLAMPS

IF IT FITS THROUGH THIS, THROW IT BACK

MEASURING RINGS

IF IT FITS THROUGH THIS, IT'S A LITTLENECK

5-gallon BUCKETS FOR QUAHOGS

CUT ENDS OF POLE TO TIGHTEN

METAL TIES

HOSE CLAMPS

12-FOOT LENGTHS OF TELESCOPIC

ALUMINUM POLE

ONION BAGS FOR QUAHOGS

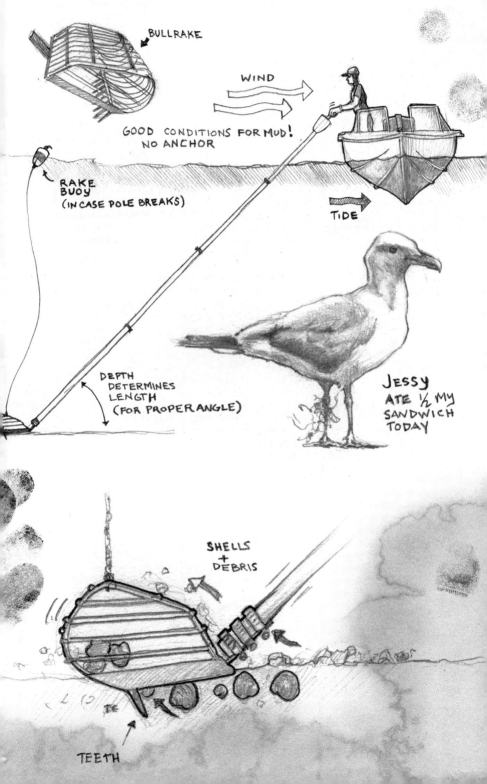

ACKNOWLEDGMENTS

We would like to thank Karen Lotz, our brilliant editor, who loved this novel from the start; Rob Weisbach, our agent and friend, who supported us with enthusiasm and poignant advice at just the right moments; and to all the hardworking shellfishermen of Narragansett Bay, who were not only our inspiration, but remain like family. Special thanks to David Parker, Greg Murphy, Bill McCagney, Greg King, D. J. Eagan, Jay Anderson, Sonny and Gene Beebe, Geoff Reilly, and Kevin Reilly. We thank our wives and daughters for helping us swim that rock: Aileen, Lisa, Alaya, Jessy, and Sophie.

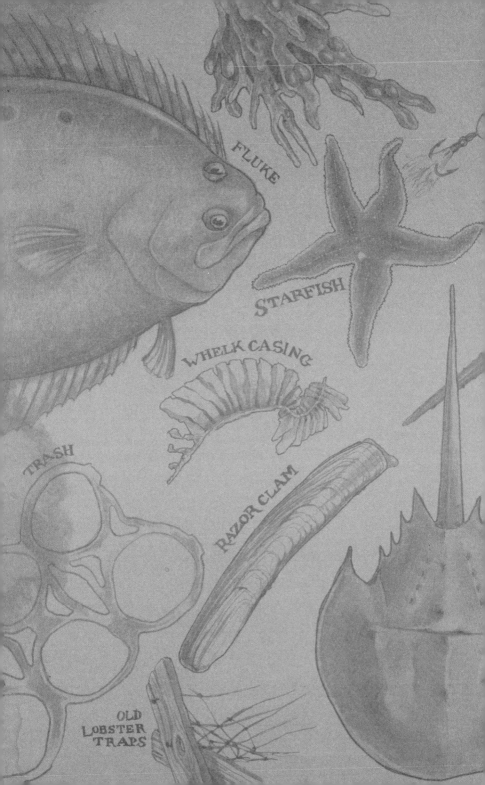

FLUKE

STARFISH

WHELK CASING

TRASH

RAZOR CLAM

OLD
LOBSTER
TRAPS